The Great Pumpkin Ride

To Mark
May all your pumpkins
shine bright!
Laura Chase
+
Sally

Other books by Laura Hesse

The Holiday Series:

One Frosty Christmas
Published, December 2003
Running L Productions
ISBN: 0-9734013-0-3

The Great Pumpkin Ride
Published, September 2004
Running L Productions
ISBN: 0-9734013-1-1

Soon to be Released:

A Filly Called Easter
Easter, 2005
Running L Productions
ISBN: 0-9734013-2-X

The Great Pumpkin Ride

By

Laura Hesse

Running L Productions
Nanaimo, B.C.

The Great Pumpkin Ride

Library and Archives Canada Cataloguing in Publication Data

Hesse, Laura - 1959
   The great pumpkin ride/by Laura Hesse

   ISBN: 0-9734013-1-1

1.Ponies-Juvenile Fiction. 2. Children with disabilities-Juvenile Fiction. 3. Halloween/Seasonal stories. Canadian (English).
I. Title.

PS8565.E84553G74 2004   jC813'.6   C2004-904499-0

Running L Productions
#9 - 2993 104th Street
Nanaimo, BC
Canada V9T 2E6
Email: *RunningL@bcsupernet.com*
www: *www.runninglproductions.com*

The author and the publisher make no representation, express or implied, with regard to the accuracy of the information contained in this book. The material is provided for entertainment purposes and the references are intended to be supportive to the intent of the story. The author and the publisher are not responsible for any action taken based on the information provided in this book.

All characters in this publication, other than those clearly in the public domain, are fictitious and any resemblance to real persons, living or dead, is purely coincidental.

Printed in Canada

To my greatest supporters,
both two-legged and four... may your
pumpkins forever light your way home...

Acknowledgments

To all those friends and family that encouraged me in my writing and who are too numerous to list here, I would like to thank you for patiently sharing my triumphs and graciously sharing my tears over the last three years. The volunteers and staff at the many Therapeutic Riding Associations on Vancouver Island and the Lower Mainland are truly remarkable people and I whole-heartedly appreciate their support. Technically speaking, where would any writer or publisher be without their editor, friend and foe (Diane and Adrian Andrews), cover designer and lay-out specialist (Linda Hildebrand, Phantom Press), and the print specialists at Friesen's...lost I am sure. May your trails be filled with beauty.

My thanks,

Laura L. Hesse

Contents

Chapter One

Harvest

Harvest Feast in River Bend is as close to Halloween in the city as a watermelon is to a fish.

There are no costumes to fuss over, no fireworks to set off, and no pillowcases stuffed with candy. Harvest Feast is a time when hay fills the barns, corn fills the silos, fields have been tilled and gardens have been emptied. Neighbors greet neighbors as if they haven't seen each other all year. Farmers' wives bake pies, can vegetables, and make jams. There is corn on the cob, roast beef, suckling pig, baked squash, candied carrots, and tarts galore. Gossip is born and new babies are coddled. Entire families get lost in the town corn maze, sing and dance to fiddle music, and eat until their zippers burst. The main events are the Pumpkin Carving Contest and The Great Pumpkin Ride.

By foot, by tractor, by wagon, and by horse, the townsfolk of River Bend make their way from the River Bend County Fairground, north along the old cliff top

1

wagon trail that borders the Athabasca River, then east into the heart of the forest where Pumpkin Alley awaits them. The townsfolk carefully light the candles nestled inside the carved out flesh of their pumpkins and place them down between the twisted roots of the ancient cedar and spruce trees that line Pumpkin Alley. Slowly they circle the lit pumpkins as night closes down upon them, admiring the talent of the carvers, young and old alike. Under the cover of darkness, they turn on their camp lanterns and make their way back to town in one long, tired procession.

Hannah Storey had refused to go to the Harvest Feast during her first year in River Bend. Despite her parent's urging, she stayed home eating popcorn and watching "The Attack of the Killer Tomatoes" on TV. She had no friends in town; in fact, the kids called her "Peg-leg" and "Gimpy-doodles", while others pretended she didn't exist. She still wasn't sure which was worse, being called names or being invisible.

Hannah had spent a lot of time laying in bed, staring at the cracked plaster on the ceiling and crying until her lungs ached and her stomach burned. She had desperately wanted to pull her Cinderella costume, the shoulders flecked with dust and two sizes too small, out of the closet and run wild down Percy Street in Edmonton yelling "Trick or Treat" at the top of her lungs. She no longer lived on Percy Street, she lived in River Bend, in a faded old farmhouse on Highway 16. She had lost touch with all her old girlfriends; none of them called or wrote to each other anymore.

This year was different. This year Hannah was going to ride her pony, Frosty, alongside Johnny Joe, and Ross and Linda McCloud in The Great Pumpkin Ride. Now, instead of crying, her hands were laced behind her head, her eyes dry, her lips pursed in a thin line of worry. She was sure Frosty had never been on a Great Pumpkin Ride either so it was going to be a brand-new adventure for both of them.

What would happen if Frosty freaked out? What if, in the dark, he stomped on a little kid's pumpkin and smashed it into smithereens? Would her friends ever talk to her again? What about ghosts? She heard there were ghosts on the Pumpkin Ride.

That didn't surprise her; she had seen several ghosts in River Bend herself. There was the girl with the baby in the house on Fourth Street. She had disappeared from the upstairs window right in front of Hannah's eyes. There were also the two fishermen who fly-fished under the bridge, their spirits drifting away with the morning fog like a dream does when one first wakes up. Yes, Hannah had seen her share of ghosts in River Bend.

When she finally fell asleep, her worries were replaced by nightmares.

She and Frosty were at the end of the last group of riders on The Great Pumpkin Ride. The ride was over and they were headed back to town. Lanterns bobbed back and forth up and down the column of riders and wagons. The night was pitch black, the stars blocked out by a thick layer of clouds. The forest appeared to be creeping in on all sides, stalking the procession like a band of woody bandits. The wind started to blow, whistling gently at first, then rising into a wild hurricane. Branches ripped off trees in great flying chunks. Lightning lit up the sky, jagged slashes that streaked from cloud to cloud, its thunderous echoes shaking the earth to its core.

Crack!

A lightning bolt struck a tree beside the trail. It exploded, snapping at the base, the top falling and narrowly missing a wagon filled with little kids in front of Hannah's group of riders. The kids screamed in terror. Frosty whinnied in fear and ran blindly into the woods.

Hannah yelled and pulled on the reins, but the pony's terror was too great! He galloped through the forest, ignoring her cries of "Whoa, Frosty!". A giant cedar seemed to pick itself up and plant itself directly in their path. Frosty slammed headlong into it. Hannah cartwheeled out of her saddle and over Frosty's back.

Hannah shook herself awake and back to reality. The school bus thumped, hitting one of the numerous potholes on the road to Cold River where she went to school. Her bottom still ached from landing on the floor beside her bed, the bus' bumpy ride not making it any better.

"I tell ya," spoke Sam Jorgenson in a hushed tone from the back of the bus. "Last year, the fog drifting in off the river was like quicksilver. It was so thick that I couldn't even see my horse's ears by the time we reached the Feed & Seed. I was never so glad in all my life as to see our truck and horse trailer."

Albert Gunnerson whispered from the bench seat beside Sam, "I saw an old trapper dressed in rags two years ago. His flesh was whiter than Ole Man Winter's hair, his eyes were as red as a Harvest Moon and he walked stooped over like he was guarding somethin' important. He walked beside us all the way out to

Pumpkin Alley and back. You ask my dad about that, see how he agrees with me?"

"I saw my Grandma, just as young and pretty as the day she got married," Ella Gunderson swore and crossed her heart.

"I saw her too," Sarah Anderson said. Sarah was Ella's best friend and seat mate. One was rarely seen without the other.

"You always see what Ella does, Sarah. You don't have no mind of your own except for what she tells ya," Sam quipped. Albert guffawed.

"That's not true, Sam Jorgenson," Sarah whined, nailing Albert to his seat with a piercing look all at the same time.

Albert shrugged and went on giggling, not caring one way or the other what Sarah thought of him.

"So how come you know what Ella's Grandma looked like when she got married? Were you there?" retorted Sam. Albert bent over sideways in his seat, gripped his sides and roared with laughter. Sam whacked him on the back just to make sure Albert didn't forget to breathe.

"Sarah's seen the family pictures on the mantle, dope head," Ella countered.

"I bet you didn't see the ghosts of those two city slicker fishermen, the ones that drowned under the bridge last May? They were dressed in red-checked jackets and green hip-waders. You could even hear the water sloshing around in the waders. They walked the whole trail with Colin McKenzie and his wife," Sarah argued.

"We all saw those two," Sam nodded, his face burning. "The whole Pumpkin Ride was talkin' about it."

"I saw them too," Hannah squeaked.

"How could you, Peg-leg, you weren't there? You were too scared. Stayed at home with mom and dad to protect you," Penny Paddington sneered, her brown freckles alive and gleefully dancing over her cheeks as if they too took fun in teasing Hannah Storey.

"No, I wasn't there, but I saw them down by the river, fly-fishing under the bridge, a couple of times," Hannah stammered. She hated how Penny always put her on the spot. "When it's foggy, you can see them quite clearly."

"Yeah, right," Penny scowled, thinking Hannah had pulled one on her.

Ella and Sarah giggled together.

"All Hallow's Eve, Halloween, Harvest Feast, call it what you will, October 31st is the night that the Dead walk with the Living," Sam finished.

The kids on the bus went quiet. Sarah's thin shoulders shook beneath her fall jacket. She was a timid girl and another favourite target for Penny's pranks. Penny liked to sneak plastic bags to school in her lunch bucket and creep up behind Sarah at lunchtime and pop them. Sarah's hysterical shrieks never ceased to bore Penny.

Hannah sat in silence, wondering who, or what, would join the Pumpkin Ride this year? She hoped it would be her Gram; she would love to see her Gram's ghost.

Hannah had lost her Gram, and the lower half of her right leg, in a car accident two years earlier. She had a prosthetic leg, a fancy one that was almost as good as the real thing. It was this that made it so hard to meet new friends. Penny Paddington was still mean, but Hannah was finding it easier to ignore her as time went on. More and more, Penny was losing interest in Hannah and picking on poor Sarah. Hannah had friends everywhere, at home and at the stables where she took riding lessons, and rarely had nightmares about the accident anymore.

"Hey, Hannah, are you and Frosty gonna compete in any of the games at the Harvest Feast?" asked Linda McCloud from the seat behind her. Linda leaned forward, her blond hair hanging over her face, her knee banging into Hannah's seat back. She tugged gently on Hannah's black ponytail. Linda was always moving, her body, her mouth, her hands, anything she could. Linda latched on to people the way that snowflakes do when they fall from the sky, more by accident than by plan.

"I'm not sure yet. I want to, but my mother is worried that I'll fall off Frosty and break my other leg," Hannah joked, reaching around and pulling her hair out of Linda's grasp.

Johnny Joe, Hannah's best friend and neighbour, chuckled, his ski jacket rustling as their shoulders touched. Johnny's brown eyes glinted and the small laugh lines that already creased the corners of his broad face arced upwards. Johnny was quick to laugh, naturally good-natured, and solid as the dark earth that supported the town of River Bend. Until Hannah came along, he was a quiet boy, keeping to himself, never fully accepted by the kids on the bus because he wasn't born in River Bend. He hadn't fit in at school with the kids from the Dènè Reservation north of Cold River either.

"Tell her not to worry. If you break your leg and Frosty won't carry you around, then me or Johnny will," said Ross McCloud, giving one more playful tug on

Hannah's ponytail just to make her laugh. Ross loved to hear Hannah laugh; it was like wind chimes in a summer's breeze. Ross was the most popular boy in school, tall, blond, handsome, and stuck on Hannah Storey.

"It won't be you carryin' around Miss Dipsy-Doodle, McCloud. She wouldn't let nobody save that ugly old nag of hers," Penny Paddington growled from the seat in front of Hannah and Johnny.

Penny glowered at Hannah, hating her for being everything that she wasn't. Hannah was small and pretty with coal black hair and blue eyes as dazzling as a mountain pool. Penny was strong-armed, coarse, big-boned, and frizzy-haired. Penny thought Hannah was the reason for every extra chore that had befallen her over the last year. It never occurred to Penny that she only had herself to blame.

"Frosty is not ugly. He's cute in a warped, flea-bitten sort of way," Linda retorted.

"Frosty isn't flea-bitten, Linda," Hannah gasped, her cheeks flushing.

"Well, he is sort'a. Don't get mad. I love him anyway, even if he does look like a tom cat who lost one too many fights." Linda giggled.

"She's got you there," said Johnny, elbowing Hannah gently in the ribs.

"Yeah. I guess it's true." Hannah smiled crookedly.

"Hey, Johnny, I bet Frosty could take Charlie Horse in the Barrel Race," Ross said. "But there's no way he could beat my Pizzazz. That mare of mine can spin on a dime and leave you five cents change."

"Well then we don't need to compete, Ross. We'll just tell the Judge to give you a First, me a Second, and

Johnny Third." Hannah pulled her hair lose from her ponytail, wrapped it back up and pulled it over her left shoulder out of the McCloud's grasp.

"That works for me," joked Ross.

"You guys are so dull." Penny sneered, "There ain't no power like tractor power. I'm goin' to drive in the Tractor Pull this year and I'm gonna win it too."

"Good on you," said Ella from the seat across the aisle.

Penny laughed, a booming sound that bounced off the walls of the bus, then stood up and sidled into the empty seat behind Ella and Sarah.

"Tractor power is real horse power," Penny finished, leaning forward over the seat and flicking Sarah in the ear with the tip of her middle finger.

"Like we care," Linda quipped.

"Shut up, Linda. You don't know nothin'. You follow Hannah around like she's some kinda Princess. Get a life," Penny fired at Linda.

Linda blushed a deep shade of red and tears rose into her eyes.

"Leave my sister alone," Ross jumped up, his lean body towering over Penny's seated form. It was his job to insult his little sister, not Penny Paddington's.

"Ross, sit down," Mrs Ellis, the school bus driver, shouted from the front of the bus.

"Yes, Ma'am. Sorry, Mrs Ellis." Ross sat back down, glaring at Penny. Ross blamed Penny for Hannah ending up in the hospital after being shot at by Ole Man Levy. He would never forgive Penny for it.

Linda sulked, then all at once, her face brightened. "You know what we should do?" she whispered, grip-

9

ping the seat back as if she were on a roller coaster in the middle of a hairpin turn.

"What?" Ross growled, still irked by Penny's attitude.

"We should have a camp-out Halloween night. It's on a Saturday this year. Mom and Dad would let us."

"That would be cool!" Hannah exclaimed. "But I don't want to miss The Great Pumpkin Ride."

"We could go after it if we set up camp that morning," Johnny suggested, warming to the idea.

"It'll be pitch black when we're done, and where can we camp?" Hannah asked, a little unsure now.

"We could use the old trapper's cabin? That's real close to Pumpkin Alley and the horses already know the way. We'll have lanterns anyway," suggested Linda.

"She's right! It's a good idea. We can clean up the cabin and clear the chimney so we can have a fire. It's pretty cold at night," Ross said thoughtfully. He leaned forward, his blue-grey eyes sparkling. "It really would be cool."

"We do already have that corral out back, the one we made for Frosty when we were goin' to hide him there last winter. It would be fine for the horses for one night." Johnny rubbed his chin.

"Well, what about it?" Linda surged forward over the seat, wrapping her arms around Johnny's neck and giving him a big hug.

Johnny blushed.

"Let go, Linda, I can't breathe," he croaked.

"Oh, sorry."

"Come on, let's do it. Our horses get along. They've spent half the summer together. Sal and Pizzazz are stable mates and so are Frosty and Charlie. If we enlarge the pen, they'll be fine," Ross added.

"It really would be neat," Hannah replied. "Exactly where is Pumpkin Alley though? How far is it from the cabin?"

"You've been there. Do you remember last winter when we snowshoed to the cabin and we hit that trail that's hemmed in on all sides by the cedar and spruce trees? It's really dark and the ground is quite swampy," Johnny said.

"You mean the wide trail behind our place that goes down to the river?" asked Hannah.

"Yeah. You call it 'Sleepy Hollow'," Johnny finished.

"That's Pumpkin Alley?"

"Yep," Linda answered.

"Oh, my," Hannah sat upright, her back rigid, and her mouth going dry. She knew that trail alright. She had gotten lost on it the first time she went hiking out behind the house. Hannah felt goose bumps rise the length of her arms.

Although her watch had said, 2:00 pm, it was like dusk inside the forest. Hannah couldn't tell north from south or east from west, the stand of cedar and spruce trees so thick that she couldn't see the sun, not even a glimpse. She was angry at herself for not knowing better than to come out here alone...she was a city kid used to street signs and cellular phones, not a country kid used to traipsing through the bush.

In the forest, time stood still, morning to night.

Which way was home? Which way should she turn?

She ran back and forth, this way and that, up the trail and down the trail. She swore that the forest was trying

11

to trap her. The trees reached out and snagged her arm like a frog on a lily pad waiting for a passing fly to "zip","zap" and "thanks for the dinner, ma'am." That was when the earth started to shake.

The Headless Horseman galloped down the trail towards her, white eyes a' blazing inside his pumpkin head. He rode a gigantic black horse that foamed at the mouth like a rabid dog. It fixed her to the spot with its angry red eyes. The Horseman raised a shiny, crescent-shaped sword over his head and bore down on her.

Hannah gasped and reached for her neck. At least this time, she reasoned, she could throw Linda in the Horseman's path. A small, but noble sacrifice so she said, "Let's do it."

"Alright," Johnny, Linda and Ross said together.

"Good idea, Sis." Ross turned and playfully punched his sister in the arm.

"Coolio!" joked Hannah and Johnny.

"Cosmo!" Linda replied.

The four of them broke out laughing.

Linda had decided that "Cosmo" was in; "Coolio" was out. Thinking that she was doing the right thing, her mother had bought Linda a subscription to Cosmo Magazine for her tenth birthday. Linda now wanted to be a model and travel to far off places. Her mother had regretted it ever since.

"Do you think it's haunted?" Linda piped up.

"What's haunted?" Hannah asked, twisting around and leaning against the bus' window. It rattled and banged behind her. The farm fields rolling by outside the window were black and muddy, the crops long since harvested, the earth turned over.

12

"The trapper's cabin, silly," said Linda, shaking her head, her blond locks bouncing. She gave Hannah a curious look, wondering why she didn't get it.

Ross and Johnny exchanged glances.

"Could be?" Ross smirked. "I doubt it though."

"Haven't you ever wondered why no trees grow in the clearing? I mean, no one looks after it and the forest is thick everywhere else but there," Linda tilted her head and looked from her brother to Johnny, then to Hannah.

"Linda's right. I knew there was something odd about that place," whispered Hannah.

"Maybe the land is cursed?"suggested Linda.

"That would make it the neatest place to be on Halloween! Maybe we'll see that old trapper that Albert was talking about or even meet some new ghosts? Boy, we'd be the talk of River Bend forever!" exclaimed Ross.

"How Cosmo is that?" Linda crowed, leaping out of her seat.

Ross yanked his little sister back down and said, "Shhhh. Do you want everyone to know?"

Linda yelped and rubbed her arms.

"No. I guess not," she said.

"Let's do it," Ross whispered back.

"Okay, I'm in," Hannah said slowly, wondering if the trapper's cabin was haunted. What would she do if it was? Would she run away screaming? Hannah knew she was tough...she had stuck it out with Frosty, stealing across Ole Man Levy's fields at five a.m. through snowstorms and cold so fierce that a couple of times her eyelids froze together, but a camp-out on Halloween Eve?

13

"I'm in too," Johnny added. "We've got three weeks until the Harvest Feast. That'll give us plenty of time to clean the cabin and make the corral bigger."

"Yessss," Linda leaned back in her seat, her blue eyes sparkling.

"Agreed. We'll ask our folks tonight." Ross rubbed a hand over the stubble of hair on his head; his summer crewcut was just starting to grow in.

Johnny and Hannah nodded.

"You keep your lips zipped, Lindy, and I'll look after it," Ross winked at his little sister.

"'Kay," she said and smiled back, knowing that her brother would never let her down.

"I'm gonna go back and sit with Sam now. Let me know if it's a go tomorrow and we'll head out to the cabin Saturday afternoon after our chores are done." Ross stood up and grabbed hold of the back of the bench seat as the bus lurched sideways.

"Sounds good," Johnny replied. "I think I can be finished by lunch."

Ross nodded and made his way, straddle-legged, to the back of the bus where he plunked himself down on the seat behind Sam and Albert.

"I hope we're not going to regret this," Hannah said, picking up Johnny's hand and giving it a little squeeze.

"Oh, Hannah. Frosty will protect you from anything and anybody," Linda scolded. It was clear she thought Hannah was a little thick sometimes. "Didn't Frosty protect you from Ole Man Levy? And didn't the old man have a shotgun in his hand? There isn't a braver pony on the face of this Earth."

14

Hannah chuckled and nodded "Yes" to every question of Linda's.

"If Frosty won't protect me from a ghost, will you?"

"Nope. I'll be jumpin' on Sal's back and heading for home. It's Frosty's and the boys' duty to look after you. I'm little, not stupid." Linda giggled.

"That's a lot of comfort, Linda." Hannah grinned and leaned deeper into the seat as the school bus slowed down on its final approach into Cold River, a series of shivers creeping up her spine, chilling her to the bone. She wondered if it was her Gram tickling her ribs, poking her in the back, trying to warn her about something. Gram always said, "Trust your instincts, girl", and "Pay attention when a ghost walks over your grave, it might have something to say". Hannah always wondered how a tingling in your ears could mean someone was walking over your grave if you were still alive to feel that tingling in the first place. All the same, Hannah was feeling that tingling now and wondered if this little adventure was a good idea? Some things are better left alone. Maybe the trees didn't grow around the old trapper's cabin for a mighty good reason!

Chapter Two

Harvest Games

Ross rode Pizzazz, his tall, elegant dappled grey Quarter Horse mare along the highway's shoulder, heading for downtown River Bend. His little sister followed behind him perched atop her cream colored Norwegian Fjord mare, Sal. Sal's bristling mane, cut short in the Fjord style, was normally white with a black stripe down the middle. Linda, however, had decided that Sal would look much faster and a lot less dumpy if she had a bright purple mane and tail. Sal's temper had been short ever since, and she walked along the road, dragging her feet, her ears pinned back in disgust.

Hannah rode her frostbitten pony, Frosty, behind Linda and Sal. Frosty tucked his nose down quickly, pulling the reins out of Hannah's hands, and stuffing his nose into Sal's purple tail, unable to resist it. Sal swung her head around every few steps and shot him an evil look. Frosty snorted with glee, enjoying this new game. Hannah watched in amusement, knowing Sal never kicked, but keeping one eye open lest the mare decide to change her mind.

Johnny pulled up the rear, sitting proudly astride his bay Quarter Horse gelding, Charlie Horse. Charlie had large, gentle eyes, a small white crescent in the middle of his forehead, and two white socks. He was a placid horse, strong and sturdy.

The group was a strange sight: two four-legged all-stars, the front-runner sleek and pretty while the one at the rear was powerfully muscled, clearly both fit for the Olympics, and a pair of misfit ponies sandwiched in the middle, one rangy and the other plump as a Christmas turkey. The result was a wave of hands, a chorus of honks, and peals of laughter from inside the vehicles that passed them on the highway. One rusty Dodge pick-up pulled in behind and followed them the rest of the way to the Feed & Seed.

The River Bend Feed & Seed sat squat and open-mouthed at the edge of town like a giant bullfrog. The loading bay was filled with men milling about, some talking about their successful harvest, others arguing over falling beef prices. They were working men with deep summer tans, short haircuts and worry lines etched permanently into their foreheads. Ford, Chevy & Dodge pick-up trucks were parked in a row below the loading dock, doors and fenders streaked with dried mud.

"Hey, Dad," Ross called, steering his mare into an empty bay and pulling up in front of his father.

"Where you off to son?" Ross' dad asked with a wink. Tom McCloud had wished he was twenty years younger when Ross had asked permission for him and

Linda to go on a Halloween camp-out. Ross had also requested secrecy; Tom took his oath of silence seriously.

"We're gonna go practice barrel racing at the fairgrounds. Hannah and Frosty have never done the barrels before so we're gonna teach them how," Linda said.

"Is that so?" said Mr Gunderson, Ella's father and owner of the hardware store. "You figure a little streak of purple glory's going to help that pony of yours run a little faster too?"

The men in the loading bay chuckled. Ross blushed a deep shade of scarlet, embarrassed for his sister and the little mare. Johnny and Hannah tried to smother their giggles, but Hannah snorted out a laugh which sounded like a honking goose, the result being that Johnny started laughing so hard that he almost fell off his horse.

"Yep. Purple Lightning! That's what Sal and I are gonna be," said Linda, undaunted by Mr Gunderson's remarks. Sal stood quietly, her ears pinned back, her head down, her face a mask of self-pity. "I might change it to orange on the 31st, it being Halloween and all, but I like Purple Lightning better than Pumpkin Sally, don't you think?"

"I swear that mare of yours is embarrassed half to death, Sweet Pea," Mr McCloud said, feeling sorry for his daughter's pony. He shook his head and smiled down at the mare.

"No, she's not, Dad, she's always grumpy when I put a saddle on her. She thinks she should just hang out and look pretty in the pasture."

"Pretty in purple," Hannah quipped as she reached out and gave Sal a reassuring pat on the neck. Sal lifted

18

her head over Frosty's back and nuzzled Hannah's hand gently.

The men on the loading dock fell silent all at once.

A truck's door slammed shut across the street. Ole Man Levy stood by his battered Dodge, returning the stare of the men in the loading dock.

The old man looked even worse for wear in jeans that hung two sizes too big for his gaunt hips, his lined face white and parched, his thin shoulders hunched forward as if he were waiting for life to kick him one more time. He wore the same red checked shirt that Hannah remembered from last Christmas and a tattered baseball cap with the words, John Deere, barely visible on the front. He was a man who didn't care how the world saw him.

The old man glared at the group of silent kids and men, then veered right towards Mom's Restaurant and Bakery.

Frosty raised his head, his frost-torn ears swivelling forward, and he snorted in anger. He swung around, slamming his rump into Charlie Horse's and his shoulder into Sal, trying to push them out of his way. Hannah reined him in sharply.

"Ow," Linda muttered, Frosty's bit catching her fingers as he lifted his head over her hands.

Johnny nudged Charlie Horse in closer to Frosty, knowing how much the little mustang hated the old man, intent on using the big bay as a road block to keep Frosty from bolting across the road. Frosty leaned into Charlie and pinned back his ears, his eyes smoldering with anger, the hairs on his neck bristling.

19

"Whoa, Frosty," Hannah said, caressing the pony's neck. Her fingers tingled, Frosty's hairs were charged with electricity. "He scares me too, but that's no reason to try and run off."

"I don't think he's scared, Hannah. That's hate in your pony's eyes. Hate worse'n I've ever seen. You keep a firm hand on him now," said Mr McCloud quietly. He squatted down on the landing and grabbed hold of Sal's reins. "Steady old girl."

Sal stood solidly in place, ignoring both Tom McCloud's hand and Frosty's pushing against her shoulder. Sal was only 13.3 hands high, but she weighed close to one thousand pounds and it took a lot to rile her up; Linda seemed to be the only one that could truly get her steamed.

Pizzazz snorted and danced sideways.

"Easy, Pizzazz," Ross said, lifting his reins and sitting deep in the saddle. Pizzazz did as commanded and settled down instantly.

The cow bell fixed above the door at Mom's Restaurant and Bakery jangled as Ole Man Levy opened the door, then disappeared into the darkness of the restaurant without so much as a glance over his shoulder. The door closed behind him with a swish and another jingle.

"Sour old man that is," Mr Gunderson said, tossing his cigarette to the ground and stamping it out with a boot heel. "He's nothing to be afraid of, Hannah. He's just gone mean and bitter over the years. Losing his wife to cancer and his cows to the bank, emptied him out."

"He still scares me, especially what he did to Mr Frost," Hannah replied, relieved that with the old man out of sight, Frosty had lowered his head and calmed down.

"Mr Frost? You mean what he did to you!" said Linda, aghast.

"Yeah! Hannah, he shot you!" exclaimed Ross.

"He didn't mean it," Hannah muttered, surprised at herself for defending the crazy old man. She hadn't known that Ole Man Levy had lost his wife that way or that he used to be a rancher. Hannah knew about grief, more so than any kid of twelve should.

"Hannah's right, kids, it was an accident or Constable Bob would have charged him," Ross' father scolded him. Ross lifted his head to argue, saw the warning look in his father's eye and decided against it.

"And he hasn't visited the hardware store to buy any firearms since," Mr Gunderson added.

"So you calling that pony Mr Frost now, Hannah?" Albert asked as he walked through the doorway of the Feed & Seed with his father. Hannah was always stunned by Albert's resemblance to his dad; they were more like twins than father and son. Both were short and lean with a tussle of auburn hair and an endless stream of freckles dancing up their arms and over their cheeks. The Gunnerson's were related to the Paddington's through several family marriages, and reminding Albert that he and Penny were first cousins often ended in a wrestling match and church chores. Albert's practical jokes had received legendary status at school and the teachers all agreed that he had surpassed his dad's record for extra school work.

"Mr Frost is Frosty's show name for when he wins the Barrel Races," Linda jumped in.

21

"I thought you and Purple Lightning were going to win the Barrel Races, Sweet Pea?" joked Linda's dad. Sal lifted her head and fixed him with a bitter look. Tom McCloud laughed and stood back up.

"Not with that hay belly, Dad," Ross quipped, then grinned.

They forgot about Ole Man Levy in a hurry. Most of the men thought he was a waste of time, no use worrying about. All of them had tried to help him out at some point of time, but had been given the cold shoulder. No one bothered anymore.

"Well, you kids have fun. Ross, you or Johnny come get one of us here if anything happens," Ross' father nodded. "I'll be here for awhile yet."

"Yes, Dad," Johnny and Ross replied together.

Tom McCloud shook his head and chuckled.

The kids backed their ponies away from the Feed & Seed and ambled by Mom's Restaurant and Grocery, keeping a watchful eye on the door incase Ole Man Levy should decide to come out. To their relief, he didn't.

The group rode in pairs down Main Street, Johnny in front with Ross and Hannah beside Linda at the rear. Cars slowed and waited patiently as the kids rode past the River Bend Grocery and Pharmacy. The store was always busy on a sunny Saturday afternoon. Ella and Sarah pushed their way out of the store holding a can of Coke in one hand and a Snickers bar in the other. The girls giggled helplessly when they saw Sal's purple Mohawk cut. Hannah and Ross waved.

The kids trotted by Gunderson's Home Hardware, the horses' shoes clip clopping on the pavement, the sound bouncing off the walls of the surrounding houses.

They rode past several empty and boarded up buildings, the paint blistered and peeling, down First and Second Avenues, then left on Third. They reined their horses to a walk and let them go at their own speed.

Unlike the downtown core, the picket fenced houses on Third Avenue showed evidence of repair. At number thirteen, a faded bungalow that backed onto the river, empty boxes were stacked in a pile in front of the garage. The young couple that just bought the house was already trying to spruce it up before winter. The pretty, very pregnant, wife waved from the front porch, a paint brush dripping with moss colored paint in her hand, half of the porch beams covered with fresh paint. Her husband looked up briefly, then continued to rake ten years worth of dead grass, weeds and leaves into a giant pile in the front yard.

Seven doors down, a retired carpenter from Edmonton was tearing down the old fence that surrounded his gabled two storey house. New cedar fence posts lay in a neat line down the middle of the driveway. He laughed and waved at the kids, happy with the life offered by a small town.

It occurred to Hannah as she rode Frosty down the lane into the fairgrounds that the Riverbenders, as she called the townsfolk of River Bend, were having to get used to a whole lot of new people moving to River Bend since she moved to town.

The Riverbenders hadn't liked Hannah or her family when they first moved to town because the Storeys were city-slickers. Her father was accepted the most; Jim Storey knew tractors, everything about them, but he still wasn't born in River Bend. Hannah and her mother didn't know one cow from another, let alone when to plant or when to harvest. The fact that Hannah was an amputee and her mother was an artist made it all the more difficult. The sounds of rock & roll blasting from their den didn't help either.

Momma Lotham, owner of Mom's Restaurant and Bakery, in a kind gesture asked Anne Storey to paint a picture of the restaurant. Momma Lotham wasn't prepared for the artist and the giant easel set squarely in the middle of Main Street, nor the tubes of paints scattered around her and the Sony ghetto blaster at her feet. The Who, Stevie Ray, and BTO rocked River Bend for four hours. Word got out and folks from all the farms and ranches in the area came to "see that crazy artist lady work". In the end, Momma Lotham made lots of money and gave her mother a one hundred dollar bonus for the picture. The painting still hung proudly on the wall behind the cash register.

"I can't believe you feel sorry for that old geezer, Hannah," Ross said as the group made their way up the dusty lane and into the River Bend County Fairgrounds.

"Why?" asked Hannah, kicking Frosty forward.

"Because he's mean and ornery," Ross responded sheepishly, his face turning red.

"You heard Mr. Gunderson. Ole Man Levy lost his wife and cattle. Think about it, Ross. Ole Man Levy's family doesn't come and see him. He lives all alone in that creepy old house. I'd be pretty angry too," Hannah added.

"Hannah, you still have a scar on your cheek from that fence pole exploding right beside your face. You were lucky that bullet hit the pole and not your head,"

24

Ross said, turning in his saddle and waving a hand in the air to make a point.

Hannah fingered the long, thin sliver of a scar on her right cheek.

"It was an accident. Besides, Frosty belongs to me now. So long as Ole Man Levy doesn't try to take him back, I can leave it alone," conceded Hannah.

Johnny reined Charlie Horse up in front of the riding ring's wide metal gate. The riding ring took up most of the fairgrounds and was used for various events. He dismounted and walked the big gelding into the ring.

"Well, you're more forgiving than I am, I guess," said Ross, dismounting Pizzazz and following Johnny into the sandy ring. "I know it ain't very Christian of me, but he's a mean old cuss."

Frosty snorted as if in agreement with Ross. The kids all laughed.

The River Bend County Fairground wasn't much. A grey cement building housed the men and ladies bathrooms and did double duty as a small concession stand. The concession stand was shuttered up, but had just received a fresh coat of paint in preparation for the Harvest Feast. The riding ring had a cattle shoot at one end and a series of small white railed corrals on the far side. That alone told volumes about what the townsfolk of River Bend considered important.

"Can we change the subject?" Linda asked, a smirk on her face.

"To what?" Johnny grinned.

"Barrel racing, of course," piped Linda.

"Sounds good to me, Lindy," finished Ross. "I'll go set up the barrels."

Ross handed Pizzazz' reins to Johnny and sauntered over to the far easterly corner of the ring, his footsteps leaving dark imprints in the sand. When he got there, he kicked over three rusty oil barrels piled along the white railing, then rolled them across the ring. He stood the first barrel at the far end of the ring, and pushed the remaining two down to the bottom. The barrels formed a triangle. Ross paced off the distance to where he thought the Start should be and scratched a line in the sand with his boot heel.

"What do you think, Johnny, this about right?" he called.

"Looks good to me," Johnny called back.

"So what do I do?" Hannah asked from atop Frosty. Frosty watched Ross' every move with intense interest, the muscles quivering in his shoulders and hind quarters.

"Well, it's a timed...," Johnny tried to say, still holding onto the horse's reins, but Linda cut him off.

"It's a timed event and you start at the line that Ross just drew, then you gallop around the barrels in a cloverleaf pattern taking the first two barrels. You race up to the third and whip straight back down to the finish line," said Linda, her hands pointing, her seat vibrating in the saddle. Sal ignored Linda, closed her eyes and went to sleep.

"Thanks, Linda," sighed Johnny. "As I was saying, you have to make sure that you cross your path or you're disqualified. If you tip over a barrel, it adds time to your score."

"That sounds easy enough," said Hannah, shading her eyes from the sun.

Ross walked back to the gate and accepted Pizzazz' reins from Johnny. He put a foot in the stirrup and swung his leg over the saddle.

"It's a hoot!" exclaimed Linda. "I bet Frosty can take Pizzazz. She gets too excited and swings too wide on the last barrel. It happens all the time."

Ross reached over and cuffed Linda behind the head.

"Hey! It's true," squeaked Linda.

"You don't need to advertise it," Ross sulked. He rolled his eyes at Hannah.

"Come on, you guys, in the ring," Johnny commanded.

Hannah steered Frosty through the gate. He pranced along the side rails, ready and willing for action. Hannah idly wondered if she could handle the little mustang. She had her hands full jumping him at her Thursday night riding lessons and sometimes wished she was still riding Groucho. Groucho was calm and quiet; he was the first pony that she had ever been on. Groucho was too small for her to jump so once she started riding Frosty, she was jumping cross-rails in no time. Frosty was thin and wiry, raw and tough.

Linda jabbed a finger into Sal's wide neck, trying to wake her up. Sal let out a long sigh, opened her eyes and ambled forward into the ring as if that was the last place she wanted to be.

Johnny closed the gate behind him and vaulted onto Charlie's back.

"Want I should run my mare around the barrels at a trot first so you can see?" Ross said, eagerly.

Hannah nodded.

The kids took their places, side by side, along the fence line, a long way from where Ross and Pizzazz were preparing to start.

Ross circled Pizzazz a couple of times. The mare snorted and skittered sideways. She was a sensitive mare, the slightest touch moving her right or left. Ross rode with an easy hand. He pointed the mare at the barrel and she reared, rocking on her haunches.

"Easy girl," Ross whispered, lifting the reins and sitting deep in the saddle.

Pizzazz settled into a fast trot, her head tucked into her chest, her white tail swishing back and forth. Ross let her trot the maple leaf pattern around the first two barrels, then as he rounded the last barrel, he let the mare loose. Pizzazz leapt forward and launched herself into a full out gallop.

"Yeehah!" Ross screamed.

"Go for it!" Johnny yelled. Charlie Horse lifted his head and whinnied softly.

Frosty danced on the spot, then sprang into the air, all four hooves leaving the ground at once. Hannah lifted the reins and grabbed hold of the saddle horn as he landed with a loud snort of pleasure, then settled down to watch Pizzazz dig a trench in the sand as she slid to a halt over the finish line.

Sal moved over a few paces, away from Frosty, then calmly started dozing once again.

Ross trotted back over to the group, a wide grin on his face. Pizzazz blew a great burst of steam from her nostrils and flicked her tail over her bum, proud of herself.

"And that, my dear, is what you call a Barrel Race," joked Ross, tipping an imaginary hat to Hannah.

"Wow," Hannah said. "I don't know if I can control Frosty like you can Pizzazz. I feel like I have a powder keg underneath me right now."

"We can put him in the Winnipeg Ballet. That was some leap he just did," Linda gasped, her eyes wide with envy.

"Give it a try. Keep Frosty at a trot like Ross did with Pizzazz, then let him rip around the last barrel if you think he needs to burn off some steam," Johnny advised. "If he feels like he's going to blow on you, then trot the whole course. We still have the trail ride to the cabin later and that will calm him down."

"Okay," said Hannah, gathering up her reins.

Hannah trotted Frosty over to the starting line. He danced on the spot as she lined him up in the center of the trench that Ross and his mare had dug. She went over the race in her mind and decided to take the left barrel first. Frosty pawed the earth, impatient.

"Go when you're ready and don't worry," Ross called out.

Hannah gave him a quick thumbs-up and released the pressure on the reins. Frosty trotted out quickly, ears up, head down. Hannah completed the first two barrels and let him canter to the third. When she crossed her trail like Ross had done, she leaned forward and pressed her legs together signaling Frosty to go forward. Frosty took off like a jet, barreling towards the finish line. Hannah screamed in delight. She sat back and yelled, "Sit on it, Frost". Frosty slammed on the brakes and Hannah grabbed the saddle horn as he spun to the right, his shoulder narrowly missing a fence post.

Johnny and Ross exchanged glances and let out a sigh of relief.

"That wasn't so bad," Ross mumbled.

Johnny quickly shushed him.

"What a riot!" Hannah howled. She rubbed the sweat from her face with the back of a hand and let Frosty prance over to the other horses.

"Told you Frosty was fast," Linda whacked Ross on the arm with the end of a rein.

"Oh, I always suspected that, Lindy," Ross winked.

"I can't get Sal to wake up," Linda finished, slapping the rein lightly on Sal's shoulder. Sal turned her head and gave Linda an evil look.

They heard the sound of truck tires on gravel behind them and turned to see who it was. Ross suspected his father had driven down to check on them, but he hadn't. Ross blanched, not sure what to make of this.

Ole Man Levy parked the old Dodge behind the entry gate. Without a word, he rolled down the truck's window and just sat there staring at Hannah and the pony.

"What do you think he wants?" Ross growled.

"I think he wants to watch me and Frosty run," Hannah replied.

"You okay with that?" Johnny asked.

"Yeah, so long as he doesn't get out of the truck, I am," Hannah nodded. "I might feel sorry for him, but he makes me nervous."

"I'll go over and say something to him if you want?" Ross finished, feeling he should do something since he was the oldest of the group. "It's pretty creepy the way

30

he's lookin' at you and Frosty, staring all bug-eyed like that."

"No. Leave it alone," said Hannah.

"You sure?" Johnny asked. "You don't have to run again. We can start for the cabin."

"I'm sure. I'll go again, then maybe we should call it quits for the day. I think Sal is ready for bed anyway," joked Hannah.

Linda sighed and shrugged, defeated. Sal snored on.

Hannah trotted Frosty back to the starting line.

Johnny stepped out of the stirrups and slid to the ground.

"What's up?" Ross asked him.

"I have a funny feeling. I don't like him being here. The hair's all up on the back of my neck," Johnny said, handing Charlie Horse's reins to Ross.

"Yeah, me too," Ross glanced over his shoulder to where the old man sat quietly watching Hannah from the driver's seat of the pick up. He still had made no move to get out of the truck or to talk to them. The old man just wouldn't take his eyes off Hannah and her pony. It wasn't natural. Ross decided he was going to ask him to leave after Hannah's run. He dismounted and was going to give the reins of both horses to Linda, then thought better of it.

"Take your time, Hannah," Johnny said, his voice trembling, hinting at the unease he felt.

Hannah nodded and let Frosty trot out. He was quicker this time, catching on to the game, and broke into a canter. Hannah let him have his head as she steered him around the barrels. He snorted, his eyes blazing, and broke into a gallop.

31

Hannah grinned, loving the wind in her face and the strength of the horse beneath her. Frosty gave to her hand and the gentle pressure on the bit, slowing his gallop when she asked. For a moment, she forgot all about the old man who was now leaning out the truck's window, gazing at her with a sour look on his face, and the fear that his gaze brought to her heart.

Hannah leaned forward over the saddle horn and let Frosty go as they rounded the last barrel. Frosty dug into the ring, sand spewing sideways like a motorboat's wake. He gave a deep grunt and lifted himself off the ground. Hannah laughed and urged him on. Head straight out, mane and tail flying, Frosty flew toward the finish line.

KA-BANG! RAT-A-TAT-TAT!

Frosty screamed and jumped sideways, spinning on his hind hooves. Hannah cartwheeled over his rump, her body crashing against the steel fence.

Pizzazz reared, pulling the reins out of Ross' grasp, wheeled around and bolted across the ring, stirrups flapping and reins flying. Charlie Horse leapt sideways, his eyes white with fear. Ross gave a sharp tug on his reins and the gelding planted his feet firmly, lifted his head and let out a deep throated scream.

Johnny ran across the ring to where Hannah lay sprawled on the ground. Frosty galloped off to join Pizzazz who was now trotting frantic circles at the far end of the ring.

Ross dropped Charlie's reins and ran after Johnny, knowing the horse would stay ground-tied as he was trained to do. "Stay here," he yelled at his sister.

32

Sal woke up with a snort and bolted forwards. Linda tugged on the reins, but Sal ignored her. She trotted over to Charlie Horse and stood by his side, not wanting to be left alone. The gate flew open behind Linda, hitting Sal in the rear, but the mare refused to budge. Linda sat atop her mare, her mouth open in a big round "O".

Penny emerged from behind the Concession Stand, a string of unused firecrackers in one hand, a Bic lighter in the other. She howled with laughter, her face a brilliant shade of red. She saw Ole Man Levy jump out of his pickup truck and charge across the ring to where Hannah was just starting to sit up. She hadn't realized it was the old man sitting in the truck and watching Hannah and the pony. What a bonus, she thought, dying to see how Hannah would react to the old man's coming to her rescue. She put the Bic in her pocket, deciding not to light the rest of the firecrackers in case she missed some action.

Ole Man Levy charged past Linda, Sal and Charlie Horse, and ran straight across the ring to Hannah. His red checkered coat flapped out behind him, and his eyes were wild with fury. By the time he reached her, Johnny was already helping Hannah sit up and Ross was kneeling at her side.

"God Bless, child, don't get up until I can check ya out, make sure no bones 'ar broken," the old man wheezed. "That darn Paddington gal. A right fool, her mother raised."

Johnny and Ross looked from the old man's angry face to where Penny Paddington jumped from one foot to the other on the far side of the Concession Stand. They saw the string of firecrackers in her hand and the empty, burnt casings at her feet. Hatred bubbled up inside Ross' breast and he forgot about the old man standing before him.

"I'm okay," Hannah muttered, gripping her head. She always wore a helmet when riding at the Running L, why hadn't she worn one today? She vowed not to do that again.

Frosty squealed and stamped his hoof in warning. He reared, snorted and galloped forward a few paces, then skidded to a halt and reared again.

"You better get out'a here, Mr Levy. That pony's coming for you," Johnny said, looking up at the old man.

"You have to use yer hands and check 'er good fer broken bones and fractures, boy. Don't let her stand up alone, ya hear? She might 'ave a concussion," Ole Man Levy said, one eye on the white pony.

"Yes, sir," Johnny replied.

The earth shook from the impact of galloping hooves as Frosty charged across the ring, reins flying, eyes wild, Pizzazz hot on his tail.

"Go! Run!" Ross shouted and stood up, waving his arms in front of his face, trying to change the horses' direction, veer them away from Hannah, Johnny and the old man.

Ole Man Levy vaulted over the fence like a man much younger than his years. Frosty slid to a stop and launched himself at the fence, ears pinned back, teeth out, his chest slamming into the top railing as he tried to take a piece out of the old man.

"Mark my words, girl. This pony's gonna kill ya. He's mean. Ya should 'ave let me put 'im down," growled the old man, taking a few steps back, out of the pony's reach.

"He's not mean," squeaked Hannah, still holding her head. "He only hates you, Mr Levy. You beat him and half starved him to death. He doesn't trust you and never will. This wasn't his fault any more than last time!"

"She's right," Johnny replied, still holding on to Hannah. "It's Penny's fault, not Frosty's."

Frosty trotted up and down the fence line, uttering a squeal, so high-pitched that it hurt the ears. Ross darted around the pony and gathered up his mare, not wanting to admit that at that moment Frosty scared him. Pizzazz snorted, her neck lathered with white foam, her chest heaving. Ross talked gently to her and she settled down.

"I'll give ya a ride home. Get 'er in my truck and ya boys can walk that crazy pony back. The girl can't ride after a fall like that," the old man offered, keeping a wary eye on the pony's teeth.

"I'd prefer if you go and get my dad from the Feed & Seed, Mr Levy," Ross said. "He told me if anything happens to go up there."

Ole Man Levy nodded. "I'll go an fetch 'im."

Frosty matched the old man's pace as he walked along the fence line and around the ring, back to his pickup truck.

"And you, young lady," the old man shouted at Penny, "yer folks are gonna 'ear about this. I'm gonna make sure of it!" He opened the door to his truck and jumped in, then sped out of the parking lot in a hail of gravel.

Penny laughed, stuck out her tongue and ran off, jumping over the broken fence of the derelict house that bordered the fairgrounds. She ran for home. She didn't

35

care if she had more chores. She was even starting to like that old nag of Hannah's. He put on a really good show.

Linda rode Sal up to Frosty and snatched up the reins. Frosty nuzzled her hand and walked obediently behind Sal as they walked over to where Hannah and the boys were. Charlie Horse stood by the gate, a cow pony taught to stand patiently if the reins were on the ground, waiting for someone to come and gather him up.

"Hannah, are you sure you're alright? That was a header," said Linda, her brown eyes bulging.

Hannah winced.

"I will be, but I definitely don't think we'll be riding out to the cabin until tomorrow."

"Tomorrow? More like next weekend," Ross said, patting Hannah's shoulder gently.

"Don't worry so much, you guys. The fence broke my fall, and I can count my fingers and wiggle my toes," joked Hannah. She straightened up and pressed a hand against her lower back where it throbbed painfully from hitting the railing. Frosty lowered his head and nuzzled her face. Hannah rubbed his cheek. "Don't you worry either," she said to the pony.

"Here comes my dad." Ross saw his father's Ford come wheeling into the fairgrounds in a cloud of dust. It was followed by several other pick-up trucks, all skidding around the corner like a bunch of out-of-control speed-skaters.

"I'll take Frosty home for you," Johnny consoled Hannah.

"Okay," Hannah whispered, her head starting to pound in time with the throbbing in her back. A light sweat broke out on her forehead.

"We'll get that Penny Paddington," vowed Linda.

"You bet," Ross echoed.

"Don't. I don't want it on my conscience," said Hannah, closing her eyes. "I thought I was being shot at again. I must have bad karma or something. Who would have thought that Ole Man Levy would come to help me?"

"Yeah, but he still thinks you should destroy Frosty," Ross said with a shake of his head. "It wasn't Frosty's fault, then or now."

"Some people just shouldn't own horses, I guess," Linda muttered.

Ross, Johnny and Hannah all looked up. The sincere look on Linda's face startled them and they burst out laughing just as Ollie Gunderson and Tom McCloud came running through the riding ring's gate, Albert Gunnerson and his father stopping to scoop up Charlie's reins and drag the gelding after them. It seemed to the kids as if half of River Bend was driving into the fairgrounds, not wanting to miss out on any part of the pre-Harvest Feast action.

"Guess you and Frosty are gonna be the talk of River Bend again," Ross mumbled, leaning over to whisper in Hannah's ear.

"Life in a small town," she groaned, wondering how her parents were going to react to *this* incident.

Chapter Three

The Old Trapper's Cabin

Ross leaned across the saddle horn, the reins loose on Pizzazz' neck, his mare relaxed and dozing beneath him. Sal stood snoozing beside her, the purple in her two-toned white and black mane mostly washed out by a week of wind and rain. The sky above them was overcast, the clouds high, the sun trying to break through the gloomy fall weather.

"Aren't you ready yet?" Linda asked Hannah, sitting on the Storeys' back porch stairs and twirling the ends of Sal's reins into knots.

"Almost," Hannah said as she tightened up Frosty's girth. "English saddles have a lot less leather on them than this Western gear. I can tack Frosty up in no time for our jumping lessons."

"Well, you're in cow country now," joked Ross. "Wait until next year when we get you on your first cattle drive; by the end of it, you'll be doin' up that cinch lickety split."

"Coolio!" Hannah smiled at Ross. "I'm looking forward to that."

"What about our camp-out in two weeks?" Linda asked.

"Oh, yeah," Hannah nodded, giving one final tug on Frosty's cinch.

"I hope the cabin isn't too messed up," added Johnny from his perch atop Charlie Horse. Charlie was perkier than Sal and Pizzazz; his head was up, his ears forward and his eyes fixed on the fields in the distance. Charlie loved a good trail ride; it was less dusty and far easier than ranch work.

"Why do you say that?" Hannah asked as she gathered up her reins and swung gracefully into the saddle. It seemed only yesterday that Hannah had needed someone to help her mount her pony.

"Well, we never fixed the door. It'll be quite gross if a bear or a pack of racoons have scat all over," Johnny finished.

Hannah grimaced. "I never thought of that."

Ross winked at Johnny. "Yep, we better take along a couple of thick wire scrub brushes for you girls to clean the floor with; otherwise, we'll all be sleeping outside."

"What do you mean 'for you girls to scrub the floor'?" Linda shouted, her face turning purple.

Johnny and Ross howled with laughter. Pizzazz snorted and skipped sideways.

"Gotcha!" exclaimed Ross.

"You boys are terrible," Hannah replied with a shake of her head. "Mount up, Linda. You were complaining a minute ago."

"Coming," Linda said, vaulting onto Sal's back. Startled, Sal lifted her head and snorted loudly.

"Wagon's Ho," Ross quipped.

"In your dreams, Cowboy," joked Johnny, spinning Charlie Horse on his haunches.

"Oh, sorry, Johnny," Ross said seriously.

Johnny burst out laughing and jogged off across Hannah's back pasture, the others following behind. The horses' heads were up, their ears and eyes forward, their steps elevated. Even Sal seemed to sense that she was off on an adventure today.

"I walked up here yesterday. It's pretty wet because of all the rain," Hannah said, moving Frosty up beside Charlie Horse as they rounded the pond. The bull rushes that surrounded the muddy water were brown stalks, the bushy seed pods at the top empty, the seeds blown away by the wind. The bull frogs were silent, asleep for the winter.

"I thought that we'd head over to the river trail at the end of your property, pick up the road to Pumpkin Alley and time how far it is to the cabin from there," Johnny said, speaking over his shoulder so Ross and Linda could hear.

"That's a good idea, sort of a dry run." Ross clucked to Pizzazz and she moved up beside Sal.

"I've got my pocket watch that Grandpa gave me. I'll time it to the minute," Linda said eagerly.

"Good thinking, Linda. That way, we'll know if we get turned around in the dark and miss the turn to the cabin. We can back-track if we do," Hannah noted.

Linda beamed.

"Do you think we should ribbon the trail from Pumpkin Alley so we know we won't get lost?" asked Hannah.

"I would, but if someone moves the ribbons, we'd be in real trouble," Johnny said pointedly.

"You mean Penny, don't you?" Linda said from the back of the pack.

Ross smiled at his little sister. "You're catching on fast, Lindy. We'd also be giving our plans away and would probably end up with a whole bunch of others joining us. I know Sam and Albert are going to be mad at me for not telling 'em about it. I can hear them whining now."

"Yeah, you're right," Hannah replied. "I never thought of that."

The group rode on in comfortable silence. They swung east at the end of Hannah's property and rode single file along the fence line. Birds twittered from the forest to their left and a pair of ravens told them off from the mossy, broken top of a dead spruce tree. The sun peaked out from behind the clouds causing steam to rise off the muddy trail.

They turned north and walked along the wagon trail that ran the length of the bluff, high above the swollen waters of the Athabasca River. The river was noisy, the water six feet higher up the bank in the last week, the current so fast that it gouged great chunks of gravel out of the cliff.

The forest ahead was dark and foreboding. The spruce trees' branches dipped down, brooding over the trail like a pack of sulky hyenas waiting for their next

41

meal. The wagon ruts were filled with puddles. The kids shivered and pulled their collars up around their necks.

As they entered the forest, the sun broke through the clouds behind them. The fields at their back glittered with millions of rainbow colored dew drops. The brilliant display of light made the bush ahead look even bleaker. The kids rode in complete silence. The sound of the river fell away and was replaced by the soft slurp of horse's hooves on spongy ground and the squeaky movement of leather.

The trail ahead grew more foul, the trees thinner and more evil looking, their bark scabby and crawling with grey fungus. Hannah found herself constantly looking over her shoulder, checking that Linda and Ross were still there. Johnny didn't have to tell her that this was Pumpkin Alley, alias Sleepy Hollow, she knew it. She listened carefully for the sound of extra hoof beats, half expecting the Headless Horseman to gallop around the next bend.

"Tell me when to start timing," Linda squeaked, her eyes big and round.

"As soon as we get to where the trail widens, you start counting," Johnny mumbled, his voice flat.

"What?" Linda asked.

"I'll tell you when," Hannah said, pulling Frosty up so that Sal was walking right beside her.

"Okay," Linda whispered.

The forest pressed in on both sides, the ground beneath the trees black and muddy. The air smelled dank from a century of rot. The horses' steps were muffled; water quickly filled in their tracks.

42

All at once, the trail became firmer and gravel strewn. Poplar trees grew in patches between the evergreens, their leaves already yellow. The poplars whispered to each other as a faint breeze ruffled their leaves.

"Start timing now," Hannah said to Linda, relieved to feel the breeze on her skin and to be away from the smell of Pumpkin Alley. Hannah wondered what it was going to be like riding through Pumpkin Alley at night. No wonder ghosts liked to join the ride. Pumpkin Alley must be filled with them, she realized. Frosty turned his head and playfully nipped the toe of her riding boot. She smiled and stroked his neck.

"It's one o'clock, right on the dot," Linda quipped.

Johnny rode another 100 paces up the trail, then reined Charlie to the right, nipping back east as the trail pitchforked. A stand of poplar replaced the spruce trees. The sun was now visible through the sparse canopy of fall leaves. Johnny wore a halo of blue black hair as he rode, his jaws relaxed, a faint smile tugging at his lips. Johnny liked the fall and the winter the best out of all the seasons.

Hannah straightened in her saddle, her shoulders aching, not realizing how far she had slumped forward on the ride through Pumpkin Alley. The forest made her feel small.

"How far to the cabin, Johnny?" Ross called from the back of the pack.

"Not far," Johnny answered.

The sun drifted in and out through the canopy of overhead leaves. It created a patchwork of light and dark shadows on the ground. The trail widened, but was blocked at the end by a patch of sharp bramble bushes.

Johnny reined Charlie through the center, lifting one foot to keep from getting snagged, then swung into the clearing. Charlie snorted loudly and broke into a trot, happy to be free of the forest.

The other kids followed and let their horses break into a trot too. Frosty kicked up his heels and shook his head as if shaking out the cobwebs.

The trapper's cabin stood forlorn and forgotten at the far end of the clearing. The logs were silver with age, the sod roof thick with weeds. A pair of swallows darted in and out of the stone chimney.

"It's twenty after one. It took us twenty minutes to get here," Linda chimed. "That's not bad."

"No. That should be easy," Ross said, swinging Pizzazz in between Frosty and Sal.

"It's going to be awfully dark," Hannah replied, wondering once again if this was a really good idea. What if the ghosts followed them from Pumpkin Alley? At least during The Great Pumpkin Ride, all the townsfolk would be there and they wouldn't be alone.

"Yeah, it will be, but the horses aren't likely to swing off the trail into the forest at night," Ross added. "They'll find their way, don't worry about that."

"Don't worry so much, Hannah. We'll have lanterns," Linda consoled her.

Hannah was embarrassed that Linda was calmer about it than she was. She was really going to have to get a grip on herself and stop imagining things before they happened.

Johnny rode straight up to the cabin and dismounted. He dropped Charlie's reins and climbed onto the cabin's porch. The porch boards creaked loudly beneath his feet. The big gelding quietly watched Johnny push open the broken door, lifting it slightly and bending it inwards so that he could get by.

"What's it like?" Hannah asked, hopping down from Frosty's back and handing the reins to Linda.

Ross stepped to the ground and handed Linda Pizzazz's reins as well.

"How come I have to hold the horses?" she whined.

"'Cause you're the youngest," Ross said.

"What's that got to do with anything?" Linda sulked.

"Nothing. That's just how it works. Ain't fair, is it?" Ross teased mildly.

"It's actually pretty clean in here," Johnny called through the doorway. "Just mice scat, cobwebs and dust."

Hannah and Ross stepped up onto the porch and peeked inside the cabin.

The cabin was bare except for the old wooden table and one mended chair that they had left in it last winter. The yellow, oiled canvas that had hung across the window lay torn and tattered on the floor beneath the window ledge, the winter winds having finally finished it off.

"We can't use the fireplace if there's a nest of swallows up it," Ross said, walking over and taking a peak up the stone chimney. "I can hear the babies chirping. It's late in the year for babies, but I don't want to disturb them. It's kinda strange actually. These swallows should have migrated by now, not be nesting."

Hannah smiled and walked over and stuck her head inside the old fireplace.

"Oh yeah. That's neat," she replied, listening to the faint chirping inside the chimney.

"You guys," Linda shouted from outside. "Pizzazz is being a jerk and I can't hold on to Frosty much longer either."

"Okay," Hannah yelled. "Hang tight!"

"We really can't hurt the babies...wouldn't be right," Ross said, nodding his head towards the fireplace.

"No, I agree, it wouldn't be," Johnny said. "I think we should just sleep in here on the floor if it rains and make a fire-pit out front so we can sleep under the stars if it doesn't."

"S'okay with me," commented Hannah.

"That's settled. I wish school was this easy." Ross smiled and headed for the door followed by Hannah and Johnny.

"About time," Linda said, her brows knitted together, her hands tangled in reins. Frosty's head was down, chomping at the last of the green grass in the meadow, nuzzle to nuzzle with Sal. Pizzazz had her head over Sal's neck and was nibbling on a strand of Linda's blond hair.

Ross slapped Pizzazz gently on the rear end. The mare let go of Linda's hair and dipped her head into Ross' hands.

Hannah smiled and took up Frosty's reins.

"Please don't leave me alone with all these guys again," Linda said, breathing a heavy sigh of relief.

"We won't," Hannah replied, giving Sal a quick pat.

The kids un-tacked their horses and stacked their saddles and blankets in a pile on the front porch. They slipped off bridles, put on halters, then let the horses loose in the meadow. Most of the grass in the meadow was brown and had gone to seed, but the horses seemed happy enough.

"Let's find some stones and dig out our fire pit first, shall we?" Ross said, his head cocked sideways.

The others nodded in agreement.

Ross counted out ten long paces from the cabin's porch. "About here should be safe? I don't think we have to worry about burning down the cabin. It's still pretty wet."

"Yeah, I think you're right." Johnny added, "And we don't want to be too far from the cabin if the weather turns on us."

Linda wandered into the clearing between the grazing horses, Hannah in her wake. They brushed aside the sharp sweet grass stalks with their feet, scouring the ground for small boulders suitable for rimming the fire pit with.

Ross walked back to the cabin and pulled a loose board from the far side of the porch. He broke it in half and sauntered back to Johnny, the old board tucked under one arm. He used the board to scrape through the withered grass, dug the end into the earth and peeled back a layer of sod. The black soil was filled with worms and white grubs. Johnny grabbed hold of the sod and peeled it backwards as Ross worked the board back and forth underneath, lifting the strip of grass upwards. The boys continued to work, sweat beading their brows, until they had a large barren circle of earth beneath their feet.

"Here's a good rock," Linda called, bending over and lifting up a medium sized stone. She cradled it in her arms, still looking down at the ground. "Look! There's a whole bunch of them and they're all laid out in a line."

47

"What?" Johnny and Ross asked, glancing quickly at each other, each wondering if Linda had finally lost her marbles.

"The rocks do look like they go off in a straight line," answered Hannah, moving up to stand beside Linda and studying the ground.

"That's too weird." Ross wiped the sweat from his brow with the tail end of his sweatshirt.

The boys wandered over and joined the girls. They stood looking down at the ground, puzzled, because it seemed the girls were right.

"You follow the line that way, Ross, and I'll follow it this way," Johnny suggested.

"Alright," Ross said.

Linda stood with the rock cradled in her arms like a baby, Hannah at her side. She watched the boys walk off in different directions.

"It's curving in a circle," Hannah noticed as Johnny started curving to the left and Ross started curving to the right as they walked around the edges of the clearing. "Why would anybody put a ring of rocks around a clear-ing?"

The boys looked up: Johnny looked at Ross and Ross looked at Johnny.

"Keep following it and let's see if we meet," Ross suggested.

The boys walked on, tracing the line of stones buried within the grass and clumps of brush. Ross scooted Pizzazz out of his path.

The boys stopped following the arc of the circle as they reached the end of their line, and stood face to face about ten feet from each other. The line of stones dipped inwards, continuing its path in another circle inside the first one.

Johnny's face blanched, his mouth creasing into a worried frown.

"What's wrong?" Ross asked, concerned.

"Linda, place that rock carefully where you found it," Johnny commanded.

"Why?" Linda squeaked, clearly attached to the rock now that she had been holding it for ten minutes.

"Just do as I say," Johnny said angrily.

"Johnny, what's wrong?" Hannah demanded, seeing the hurt in Linda's eyes as she returned the rock to its place.

"Hannah, walk into the middle of the clearing and see if there is a pile of stones there," Johnny said, his voice sharp.

It wasn't like Johnny to get angry. Hannah had never seen him like this before so she did as she was told, sure that there was a good explanation.

Hannah walked slowly into the center of the meadow, her eyes on the ground, searching for a pile of rocks. She stubbed her toe, crouched down and felt several rocks all jumbled together under a thick layer of grass and earth. "I think this is it."

"Okay," Johnny said, softly. "Let's go sit down and I'll explain. Linda don't touch any more rocks."

Johnny walked slump-shouldered to the trapper's cabin and sat down heavily on the porch. He leaned one arm over his saddle and wiped the sweat from his eyes with the back of the other. Ross stood before him and the girls sat down on either side.

"What is it?" Ross asked quietly.

49

Johnny smirked and looked up. "It's a Medicine Wheel. It's Blackfoot, and it has to be very, very old!"

"What's a Medicine Wheel?" Linda piped, her tears drying up and her eyes turning into gleaming diamonds.

"It's sacred ground!" Johnny said, fixing Linda to the spot with a piercing look.

"That's why the trees don't grow here, isn't it?" Linda said, her hands wheeling through the air, nearly clipping Johnny in the side of the head.

Johnny leaned sideways, away from her flailing hands.

"It's not just sacred, it's powerful. Medicine Wheels are used by the Blackfoot for several reasons. They can mark the burial place of a great warrior or chief, mark out a territory, or be used as a gathering place to conduct special ceremonies. That's what worries me," confessed Johnny.

"What is so strange about this one?" Ross asked, glancing over his shoulder at the meadow where the horses were still grazing peacefully.

"Number one, it's too small. Medicine Wheel's are usually the size of one or two football fields. Secondly, it's Blackfoot. As far as I know, the Blackfoot never traveled this far north and that means that it can't be a ceremonial place or a territory marker, so it must have been put here to mark the burial place of a very important chief. The stones in the middle probably covered the chief's body so that when the body rotted away, the rocks fell down and formed that little mound that Hannah found. All the other Medicine Wheels are in Red Deer, on the South Saskatchewan River, normal Blackfoot territory. Thirdly, if this Medicine Wheel is as old as I think it is, then it was made at a time when the Blackfoot and the Cree were mortal enemies. In case you forgot, I'm part Cree, " Johnny said earnestly.

Ross, Hannah, and even Linda sat in stunned silence.

"How Cosmo is that?" Linda muttered, wide-eyed.

"Linda," Ross said, crossly.

"Do you think that's what happened to the trapper and his family? Maybe they got cursed for building the cabin so close to the Medicine Wheel?" Linda asked, ignoring her brother's ugly stare.

"Could be," Johnny pondered.

"Maybe it's not a good idea to camp here?" Hannah whispered.

"I don't know," Johnny replied, glancing in her direction.

"Oh, come on, you guys. You said that it's ancient, Johnny. I'm sure there aren't any ghosts here. I don't really believe in them anyway," Ross said calmly.

"What about the Holy Ghost?" Linda asked her brother, startled.

"That's different," Ross quipped.

"Why? Because it's in the Bible and Medicine Wheels aren't?" Hannah said, her voice rising in anger.

"That's not fair! That's not what I meant!" Ross pulled back.

The air was thick with tension. Johnny and Hannah both glared at Ross.

"Well, I believe in ghosts and the Holy Ghost! I don't think you need to worry though, Johnny. You're only one quarter Cree and the other half is Salish from your mom's side of the family and they live mountains away from here. I'm sure the Blackfoot ghosts will be okay with that," Linda said.

Ross snorted with amusement.

Johnny and Hannah burst out laughing. Johnny gave Linda a quick hug. Linda threw her arms around his neck and planted a wet kiss on his cheek.

"Your goose is cooked now," Ross said.

"So are we doing this camp-out together or am I gonna have to do it by myself?" Linda retorted.

The kids all giggled.

"No, Linda, you won't be alone," Johnny said. "We'll all be here. I'll get my mother to make us up some medicine bundles to protect us from the ghosts. Is that fine by you?"

"Cosmo," Linda quipped.

"How about Johnny and I work on making the corral bigger? You two girls can go look in the brush beside the trail for some rocks to circle the fire pit with and leave those others alone," Ross said, pointing in the direction of the Medicine Wheel.

"That sounds good," Hannah replied, standing up. She gave Ross a pointed look, one eyebrow raised, making it clear that she thought he owed Johnny an apology.

"Come on, Linda, let's go dig for rocks," she said, gathering Linda up from her perch on the porch. The girls wandered off towards the trail they rode in on.

"Sorry, Johnny," Ross volunteered, his face turning a bright crimson. "I didn't mean anything against your beliefs."

"I know." Johnny grinned. "Mom calls me Hollywood Joe sometimes."

"No way!" Ross laughed.

"I got so used to playing the Indian kid at school before I got to know you guys that sometimes I forgot who I was," Johnny confided, surprising himself by the admission. He was sure Ross deserved his trust and would not think less of him for what he had to say.

Ross looked startled.

"So are you saying that you might come to church on Sunday?" Ross teased.

Johnny stood up, tugged down his sweater, and started ambling toward the back of the cabin where he and Ross had made a small pole corral last Christmas. Ross walked beside him. They were a strange pair: one short, broad shouldered, raven-haired and bronze-skinned, the other tall, lean and fair as a sunny day.

"No. You're Seventh Day. I'm Catholic."

"You're kidding?" Ross said, stopping dead in his tracks.

"Nope," Johnny finished.

"How did that happen?" Ross huffed and shook his head, never figuring that anyone could have more than one set of beliefs.

Johnny roared with laughter.

"My grandfather's name was Jean-Paul Joseph: his father was French Canadian and his mother was Northern Cree. He was Métis. Métis' couldn't own land at that time so my grandfather joined the army during World War Two and changed his name to Johnny Joe. He turned his back on his Heritage, but not his church. My dad joined the military too, that's how he met my mother. He was stationed on Vancouver Island and a friend of his dragged him to a Potlatch dinner where he met my mom. My dad wants me to join the military, but my mother is against it. She says too many Joe's have lost their way. That's why this Medicine Wheel worries me so much. It's like I was supposed to find it. I don't know if the Grandfathers are giving me a warning or trying to teach me a lesson. The Pumpkin Ride can be freaky enough let alone coming to a place like this that shouldn't even exist."

"Wow," said Ross. "I thought my family was cool because we have a Bible that's been in our family for three hundred years, but you got us beat. If you really think we shouldn't camp here on Halloween Night because this Medicine Wheel is kinda the same as Stone Henge to the Druids, then I'll back you if you want to cancel out."

Johnny shook his head. "No, I have to do this. We would never have found this Medicine Wheel if Linda hadn't talked us into this camping trip. Hannah, she knows about these things, but she gets scared easy. She sees things that other people can't. My mom says that she's gifted, but I don't think Hannah sees it that way. She dreams about a lot of things, and the dreams frighten her. Let's not tell her or Linda about this conversation, okay?"

"I won't." Ross admitted, "I don't want to freak Hannah out. Linda will yap it up all over school. I'm surprised that she hasn't told her girlie friends in class about our plans yet."

"Thanks," Johnny said.

Ross nodded, case closed, conversation over, and picked up a fallen fence pole, his face a dark mask of concentration.

54

Chapter Four

Halloween at the Running L

Tom McCloud swung his Ford pickup truck and stock trailer into the gravel parking lot of the Running L Riding Academy. He pulled up in front of the steel sided indoor arena and whistled loudly.

"Boys, that is one big arena," he said, looking up through the truck's windshield at the huge white building with the exhaust fans on the roof. He could hear the buzzing of the fans, the blades in constant motion, over the rough purr of his truck's diesel engine.

"Haven't you ever been here before, Mr McCloud?" asked Hannah from the back seat of the crew cab.

"No, honey, this is a first for this farm boy," he said, marveling at the scene before him. Two long, low barns were attached to the arena, each with individual turn-out paddocks for the horses. A third barn was located close to the house, the ranch house's porch overlooking its turn-out corrals. The three-tiered fencing that enclosed and cross-fenced the property was painted pearly white. "I don't think I've ever seen a spread like this before. The horses here must think they're royalty. I bet I wouldn't mind living in one of their stalls."

"Yeah, it floored me when I first saw it," Johnny replied. "Wait until you see the barns. Slick and neat, clean as a whistle, stable mats in every stall, and hot and cold water in the tack room."

"Cosmo," Linda chimed, leaning forward and resting her chin on the back of her father's seat. She rolled her eyes at Hannah. Hannah grinned back.

Tom McCloud pulled the truck around and parked close to the first barn's doors. Hannah had already told him that was the "pony barn" and that stalls had been arranged for the horses for the day.

"All-righty kids, hop out and unload your ponies. Your mothers are bound to be here with your costumes soon and we're running a bit behind," Tom said as he popped open the truck's door.

"Yes, sir," the kids replied.

The group of teens hopped out of the truck as Tom McCloud unlatched the back of the stock trailer. Pizzazz and Frosty let out a chorus of shrill whinnies which were answered by a series of muffled calls from within the stables. Charlie banged his front leg against the side of the trailer, eager to be out and to be exploring his new surroundings.

Ross went in and untied Pizzazz. His father took the mare from him and lead her over to the barn door. Ross then gave Sal to Linda, Frosty to Hannah and lead Charlie Horse out last.

"Put the horses in their stalls then come and get your tack real quick," Tom McCloud ordered, "or you're gonna miss the first event."

"Okay, Dad." Ross took his mare's lead rope from his father's hands and pulled open the barn door.

"Whoa!" Ross' eyes grew large as he led Pizzazz into the barn. The mare snorted and danced forward.

"How Cosmo is this?" Linda whispered, crowding in on Ross and Pizzazz. Sal pricked her ears up and lifted her tail, her freshly painted Halloween orange Mohawk bristling as she sashayed into the barn like a young filly.

Hannah lead Frosty past them both and walked him down the wide aisle to his stall. A piece of paper was fastened to the front with his name typed in bold red letters. The stall mats were swept clean, hay filled one corner and the water bucket had been freshly scrubbed. The water bucket was overflowing with crystal clear water. There were three other similar stalls for Pizzazz, Charlie Horse and Sal.

"Let's go guys," she said.

Johnny lead Charlie into the stall beside Frosty, a wide grin plastered to his face. He knew what Ross and Linda were feeling. He had reacted the same way the first time he had come to watch one of Hannah's riding lessons.

Hannah removed Frosty's halter and waited for the others to get their horses settled. Frosty whinnied a greeting at Groucho, the black mustachioed pony stabled directly across the aisle from him. He and Groucho were good friends, their friendship pleasing Hannah greatly since Groucho was the first pony she had ever ridden.

"Hannah, this is really cool," Ross said, shouldering past his mare as she tried to dash past him and out the stall door. Pizzazz nipped Ross' jacket. Ross was used to the mare's moods and ignored her much the same as he ignored his little sister's chatter.

"Hi, Hannah," yelled a tall, lanky red-haired girl from the end of the barn. "Glad you made it!"

"Wouldn't miss tonight. Are you the one we have to thank for the clean stalls?" Hannah called back.

"Of course. It's always a pleasure to have visitors. I'll come help you bring your tack in," Jenny said as she walked down the aisle, her soft orange hair swinging gently over her shoulders. Jenny sported a long black cape with golden moons and suns painted on the lapels. A tall pointy wizard's hat was tied to her head with black ribbon and her riding boots were so polished that they reflected the glow from the ceiling lights.

Ross saw her and his mouth fell open.

Hannah covered her mouth and giggled. She knew Ross was sweet on her, and hoped that when he met Jenny, things would change. It was getting really embarrassing at school, and Johnny and he were starting to quarrel.

"Ross," Hannah whispered, "close your mouth."

"Huh?" he said, his cheeks reddening.

Johnny left Charlie's stall, saw Ross standing there with his arms down and a goofy grin on his face, his eyes fixed on Jenny Weatherspoon, and smothered a laugh.

"Who are you?" Linda piped, closing Sal's door.

"I'm Jenny Weatherspoon and who are you?" Jenny asked back, her eyes glinting with mischief.

58

"Linda McCloud. Pleased to meet you," said Linda, politely. She turned and poked her brother in the side with one finger. Ross didn't even notice.

"Hi, Jen," Johnny added.

"Hi, Johnny," Jenny winked.

"This is Ross, Linda's brother," Hannah advised Jenny. The barn door swung open and Hannah's mother and father jogged in accompanied by Johnny's and Linda's parents, their arms filled with bridles, horse blankets and the rest of the kids' costumes.

"We better move it," Hannah said, taking the bridle and saddle blanket from her mother and throwing the blanket over the stall door. Anne gave her a quick hug and dashed back out the door for another armload of supplies including her pencils and sketch book.

"Linda, why don't you stay and help get these blankets organized and I'll bring in your saddle?" Jenny offered. Linda nodded. Jenny then joined the others as they went to gather the saddles from the back of the truck.

Ross handed Linda's saddle down to Jenny. Jenny smiled. He picked up his own and jumped out of the truck, not bothering to see if Hannah or Johnny wanted his help.

"I bet you Ross is gonna fall flat on his face shortly if he doesn't stop looking at Jenny and watch where he's going," Johnny noted.

Hannah elbowed Johnny sharply in the side. "Don't be nasty," she whispered into his ear.

"I won't. I understand how he feels; Jenny's really pretty," Johnny whispered back, teasing Hannah. Hannah smirked.

When the gang finished tacking up their horses, their mothers descended on them, fixing costumes, fussing with pins and make-up until they were satisfied that their children looked as ugly as they could be without scaring the horses.

"Come on, Hannah, rock 'n' roll," Betty Warren howled as she ran down the aisle, her cowboy boots clicking, the cowboy hat tied around her neck bobbing against her back. "The Relay's about to start!"

Hannah rearranged her witch's robes, pulled her hair back into a ponytail and straightened her pointy witch's hat. Her face itched from the green grease paint her mother had smothered on. Stray pieces of hair stuck to the paint on her cheeks. She flinched when she saw her reflection in the water bucket; she was ugly!

"Which race?" asked Hannah.

"The Relay Race and I'm short a partner because Julia came down with the flu," Betty replied. She stood with her hands on the six guns fastened to her hips, an angry smirk on her face. "Me and Jiminy Cricket can't ride without a pardner," she drawled.

"I'll ride with you," Linda said, hauling Sal out of the stall.

"Wow, are you ever bright!" Betty exclaimed.

Linda was orange! She was orange from head to foot, arms and legs, all except for the little green cap on her head which served as a pumpkin stalk. The bulging crepe paper costume crinkled when she moved. Linda had colored Sal's mane and tail with orange food coloring and had wanted to dust the mare with orange chalk, but her mother had forbidden it.

"Isn't Sal just Cosmo?" Linda squeaked. "I'm calling her Pumpkin Sally for today!"

"Super cool," Betty agreed. "Let's rock."

Linda and Betty dashed down the hall, a cowgirl and a pumpkin, with one blond and orange pony jogging behind them.

"Watch out for Jiminy Cricket, Linda. He bites, bucks and kicks," Hannah called out a warning.

Linda waved a hand over her head, but kept on running.

"Will you pardner with me?" Ross joked with Jenny, his face brightening. "We're both dressed as wizards, seems only right."

"Sure," Jenny agreed, her face flushing. "My horse, Pride, is in the arena. My mother is holding him."

Ross glanced briefly at Hannah, one eyebrow raised as if asking permission. Hannah grinned and nodded. Ross let out a sigh of relief.

Hannah had to admit Ross looked quite handsome in his blue velvet cloak, tall black boots, black jeans and wizard's cap. He had a makeshift wand tucked beneath his belt. It was spray painted silver and had a hawk feather at one end.

"Guess that means Hannah's with me," Johnny said as he lead Charlie Horse out of his stall.

"Neat!" Jenny exclaimed. "I take it you're the hunter and he's the game?"

"Yep."

Johnny had used a homemade grease paint mix that his mother had made to paint Charlie with black and white zebra stripes. Johnny was dressed in a green khaki uniform with a red bandanna tied around his throat and

61

a fake wooden shotgun over one shoulder. He didn't bother to throw a saddle on Charlie, but carried it to one side, suspecting that they wouldn't let him ride without it.

"I think you're a shoo-in for Best Costume," Jenny offered.

"Let's go, you guys," Hannah finished.

The group made its way to the arena where a dozen volunteers met them at the gate. Pictures were snapped before costume hats were replaced by helmets. Johnny was told to saddle up and he did so without protest.

The stands around the indoor ring were filled with parents, sisters, brothers, grandparents and friends. Cameras flashed. The mouth watering smoke from bar-bequed hamburgers and hot dogs filled the air.

The sides of the arena were filled with horses, costumed kids and adults. There were clowns and cowboys, Frankensteins and white sheeted ghosts, and witches and warlocks. Everyone was dressed for the event. Each new entrant that came into the arena was greeted by a round of cheers and hearty applause. No one was left out.

Linda and her pumpkin outfit were a great hit! There were screams of laughter and shouts of glee. Sal swished her fanny and arched her neck, reveling in the applause. Linda and Betty Warren were picked first for the Relay Race.

Because all the kids and adults at the Running L had different skill levels and abilities, the Relay Race was slightly different for each class of rider. It was designed so that no one would be left out. The independent riders and those with better riding skills rode first. They had to ride a timed event, while others were judged on their riding ability and horse handling skills. The main goal of the games was to have fun.

Linda gripped a tennis ball in one hand. She had to ride down the arena, put the tennis ball in a bucket atop a large white barrel, pick up a bean bag from the same barrel and ride through a gate with a secret password that she was given at the start, walk over a low wooden bridge, put the bean bag into a another bucket, then find her way through a maze. The maze had been chalked out on the arena floor. She had to pick up another tennis ball in the middle of the maze and hand the ball to Betty at the end of the course. Betty had to complete the same course. The girls times were combined for a final score.

The on-lookers screamed encouragement from the stands.

Linda nodded at the Judge and crossed the starting line. The first part was easy. They entered the maze and Linda found the tennis ball, picked it up, but couldn't figure out which way to go. She halted Sal and looked around, puzzled. She shrugged and grinned, completely lost. The kids on the sidelines yelled out wrong directions, all in fun. Linda tried a couple of them and ended up back at the barrel in the middle of the maze.

"And this is how you don't win the Relay Race," Mrs Troughton's voice boomed from an overhead speaker.

The stands erupted in cheers.

"Come on, Linda, go right! Can't you see it?" Betty screamed from atop her grey pony, Jiminy Cricket.

"No," Linda yelled back. "I'm totally lost!"

"Go right, then left, then left again," Betty screamed louder.

63

Linda laughed, followed Betty's directions and made her way out of the maze. She reined in beside Betty and tossed the tennis ball to her as Jiminy Cricket backed into Sal and lifted his left rear leg for a well placed kick. Sal jumped sideways and snapped her teeth at the grumpy gelding. The tennis ball bounced off Betty's helmet and into the stands.

Curly haired, six year old Emma Peters caught it and tossed it back into the ring without thinking. A volunteer picked it up and quickly handed the ball to Betty who then finished the course.

Linda and Betty screamed with laughter and trotted back over to join Johnny and Hannah. Betty was lucky. Jiminy Cricket wasn't a very popular horse and she didn't have to share him with anyone else so she was able to stay up on him. Mrs Troughton had thought of selling Jiminy as his bad temper made him difficult to deal with, but Betty had burst into tears so she had relented and kept him at the stables.

To even-up the game even further, Mrs Troughton decided that some of the independent riders would walk the course with side-walkers and a horse-handler. The rider would hold the tennis ball in one hand while balancing an egg on a spoon in the other. If they dropped one or the other, they would have to wait for a volunteer to give them back the egg or the ball, count to ten, then proceed. Ross and Jenny as well as Johnny and Hannah were in that category.

Ross and Jenny's numbers were drawn to go before Hannah and Johnny's. Pizzazz scooted sideways, not used to having two people walk on either side of her. She liked both her side-walkers and kept stopping for a cuddle. She stopped and cranked her head around causing Ross' egg to roll off the spoon. A volunteer bolted across the ring, picked the dirty egg off the arena floor and handed it back to Ross. Ross' face grew redder every time the egg fell off the spoon and landed with a thump in the dust.

"I think I've got egg on my face," Ross joked to the crowd in the bleachers as he handed over the tennis ball and the egg and spoon to Jenny. She laughed merrily and began her course.

"Wow, that was tough," Ross whispered to Hannah over his mare's shoulder as Hannah practiced balancing her egg on the spoon. His face grew thoughtful as he looked around at the participants and their horses. "I don't know if I'd have the guts to get on a horse with all these people around if I needed that much help. I don't know how you did it, Hannah! It must have been hard!"

"No harder than learning to walk again with this prosthetic leg of mine. It's all balance and practice. It's the guys in the wheelchairs that I find incredible. See that girl over there, the one dressed like an elf, with the white stockings? See how she rides in the saddle, her legs hanging down with no stirrups and no side-walkers. If you watch, her legs swing loose; she can't move them because she's paralyzed from the waist down. She is seriously amazing! It took her years, but she did it. There are no attitudes here. Everyone is normal," Hannah whispered back, a glint of mischief in her eye.

"I guess," Ross said quietly, his face somber, then he switched his attention back to the ring in time to see Jenny's egg roll off the spoon, bounce off her side-walker's head and roll under her gelding's hooves. Pride

65

stepped on it and the egg shattered. Ross roared with laughter and gave Jenny a thumbs-up from the sidelines. Jenny was handed another egg, finished the course, then rode over and joined Ross.

"You're next Hannah. It's much harder than it looks," Jenny shook her head. She giggled and winked at Hannah before dismounting.

Hannah and Frosty began the course. Frosty sensed Hannah's nervousness and behaved well, stepping very gingerly into the maze with Jenny's mother leading him forward on a lead line and one side-walker on the inside only as Mrs Troughton had ordered.

Hannah had a terrible time balancing the egg on the spoon. It was so bad that the kids in the ring started counting each time the egg fell into the dirt. Hannah finished the Relay Race with an egg count of twenty-eight and her face streaked with tears of laughter. She waved and bowed to the judges at the end of the Maze.

"Hannah, I think we're going to add that egg and spoon into your lesson," Mrs Troughton cackled over the speaker. A couple kids from Hannah's riding class howled with glee. Hannah's parents waved at her from the top row of the stands. Her father pulled out a handkerchief and dabbed the tears from his eyes.

"As a matter of fact, I think I'll add it to all the classes," Mrs Troughton finished.

The arena was filled with a chorus of groans.

Johnny gathered up the ball, the egg and the spoon from Hannah, then made his way around the course without dropping the egg once. His efforts tied he and Hannah for last place with Ross and Jenny.

"I think that you've lost Ross to an older woman," Johnny nudged Hannah.

"I think so too," Hannah answered. "They look pretty cute together."

Ross and Jenny were all eyes for each other. They laughed, head to head, and shared a hot dog.

Betty and Linda ended up winning first prize in their division. They waved their blue ribbons in the air and split the small gift basket of horse treats between Sal and Jiminy Cricket. Johnny and Charlie Horse won first prize for Best Halloween Costume just as Jenny had predicted.

The Halloween games at the Running L ended with Tom McCloud inviting all the folks there to come and enjoy the River Bend Harvest Feast.

"I'm sure you'll all have just as much fun in the River Bend Corn Maze as you did here," he predicted. "And I guarantee your stomachs will be just as full. We'd sure love to have your help with the fair, Mrs Troughton, if you will do us the honor. You run quite a show." The invitation was met with thunderous cheers and clapping.

Chapter Five

Harvest Feast

"It's official! We've broken all attendance records and it's not even supper time," Pastor Smith roared over the loudspeakers. The crowd inside the River Bend County Fairground howled and clapped.

"Welcome one and all, especially you folks from Cold River, Knob Hill and all points north, west, east, south and beyond. How about a big round of applause for Mrs Dorothy Troughton, the owner of the Running L Riding Academy, who has volunteered to help co-ordinate the Barrel Race today. She's got a big job ahead of her folks," Pastor Smith finished.

Mrs Troughton waved a hand over her head from her position in front of the arena's in-gate where at least one hundred kids and their ponies waited outside for their number to be called. A thunderous round of applause shook the stands that circled the riding ring. Mrs Troughton's stiff posture broke for a moment, and she blushed a deep shade of crimson.

The fairground was a sea of people and animals. 4H pens were filled with chickens, pigs, cattle and sheep, the wide-eyed kids that owned them vibrating, hoping that they'd win Best in Breed ribbons. Long, lace covered tables overflowed with pies, cakes, and tarts of unimaginable variety. Colossal squash, pumpkins, and eggplant sat beside row on row of canned fruit and pickled vegetables. Judges in starched white shirts, blue jackets and black slacks, each with a gold "Judge"pin fastened to their lapel, roamed from table to table and pen to pen. They carefully scored the entrants in each category, their faces set in stern scowls, their job taken as seriously as any Supreme Court Judge's.

The air was alive with fiddle music, laughter, and animal sounds. Thin lines of mouth-watering smoke drifted skywards from two huge BBQ pits as fat dripped on the coals from several spits of roasting beef and suckling pig. Hamburgers and hot dogs sizzled over smaller fires. There was food, livestock and smiling people everywhere one looked.

The corn maze was located in the field behind the fairgrounds. The Alberts were responsible for sowing the corn and designing the maze this year. Dozens of their family members manned the entrance and the exits to the maze. Several of them sat on lawn chairs within the corn field, eager to help lost kids find their parents and to keep teenagers, young and old alike, from getting into trouble. Mrs Troughton brought a group of volunteers from the Running L's Therapeutic Program as well as three ponies. The ponies, Groucho included, were already mounted with happy riders, side-walkers at their posts beside them, families gathered at the entrance, all set to head into the maze together.

Over by the arena, the Barrel Racing had quickly become "The Main Event" as the list of entrants topped 118. The Tractor Pull, usually held in the ring after the Barrel Racing, was moved to the rear parking lot because of all the entries.

The Barrel Racing was broken down into extra categories: Children 6 and Under (accompanied by parent, brother or sister), Youth 7 - 10, Junior Teens 11 - 15, Adults at 16 and Up. "Children 6 and Under" was a new category. The youngest rider, little Allie Thompson, three years old and hanging onto the saddle horn for all she was worth rode her thirty year old pony named "Boomer" across the finish line with a time of 4 minutes, 32 seconds. Boomer never once broke out of a slow, head-bobbing walk no matter how hard Jenna, Allie's older sister, pulled on his lead rope or little Allie kicked. Allie won a blue ribbon, much to the crowd's delight, just for making it around the course. Jenna was awarded a red ribbon for coaxing the stubborn pony across the finish line by waving a carrot in front of his nose.

Johnny and Hannah had already ridden the horses in the warm-up area. Frosty was a handful; he bucked his way around the sandy enclosure, scattering horses and riders in every direction.

"You don't have to run the barrels just 'cause we are, Hannah, " Johnny said, noticing they had the ring to themselves. "The Pumpkin Ride might be enough for Frosty."

"I know. I'm scared, I won't lie, but I'm going to do it, Johnny," Hannah answered. "Frosty's got some of my nerves, that's all. I didn't realize that there would be so many people here."

"The pastor wasn't kidding about the record being broken. I used to know everyone at the fair, but not this year."

"Let's go watch Linda and Sal; they're bound to be called soon," Johnny offered.

Hannah dismounted and walked Frosty out of the ring. He pranced beside her. Several riders nodded and rode back into the warm-up ring, glad that the little mustang was leaving.

Johnny sat astride his gelding, calmly eating a corn dog while waiting for his class to begin. Charlie Horse rested one hind leg and napped beneath him.

Hannah stood beside Johnny and Charlie, holding tightly onto her pony's reins. She stroked his neck gently. Frosty's ears flicked back and forth, his eyes bright, his pink nostrils flared, his head swivelling this way and that, watching the crowd and the ponies in the ring. The hairs on his neck quivered.

"Number 46, Linda McCloud riding Purple Lightning," the pastor called out, then broke into a hysterical fit of giggles as they entered the arena. The loudspeaker crackled and squealed.

"Go, Linda! Go, Sal!" Hannah yelled.

"It's Purple Lightning, not Sal," Linda hollered back.

Mrs Troughton started chuckling from her post at the gate.

Linda and Sal, alias Purple Lightning, trotted the barrels, Sal's purple mohawk bobbing, the purple ribbons in her tail fluttering out behind her like a lavender bridal train. The crowd clapped and screamed, "Purple

71

Lightning!". It was evident by the wide grin on Linda's face that she didn't much care if she and Sal won a ribbon. Linda knew Sal wasn't fast, but she also knew her mare could outlast and outwork any of the horses at the Fair during branding time. Few kids received the good morning whinny and hug every morning that Sal gave Linda. They placed a dismal 27th out of 34.

Ross missed his sister's ride. He and Jenny were off in the corn maze

"Youths, 10 - 15, get your horses ready," Pastor Smith announced.

"I hope Ross makes it back in time," Hannah said to Johnny. "Where's Pizzazz?"

"He'll make it," Johnny mumbled. He licked his fingers, wrapped a napkin around the corn dog stick and put it in his pocket. "I can see Linda warming up Pizzazz in the warm-up ring and Betty's having a hoot riding Sal alongside her. I swear that mare of Linda's has a smile on her face. Ross won't be late; he has a good reason to win today."

Hannah grinned.

"You're being wicked, Johnny," she teased.

Johnny smiled down at Hannah.

"Well, he and Pizzazz have got to show off for Jenny. He's gonna be tough to beat, don't you doubt it. If he lets that mare go, she's gonna fly! What you saw a couple of weeks ago was nothing."

"That make you nervous?" Hannah asked, her eyes bright.

"Nope. Charlie's no slouch and neither is Frosty. Sam's here with that big buckskin he just bought. I think that gelding's got some speed in him. Did you see those haunches?" Johnny shook his head and shifted in the saddle, then gave Charlie Horse a pat.

"You guys really take these games seriously," Hannah said, putting her foot in the stirrup and swinging into the saddle. Frosty skipped sideways into Charlie. Johnny put out a hand to steady him as a lady with a stroller walked by on the other side.

"Rider 72, in the ring. Number 73, next!" Mrs. Troughton hollered from the in-gate.

"73. That's you, Johnny," Hannah moved Frosty over.

"Yep and yep!" Johnny grinned. "Time to roll." He tipped his cowboy hat to Hannah and moved Charlie into position as rider 72 went into the ring. Rider 72 rode a little Appaloosa mare, lean and mousy, with a mean disposition. Johnny kept well back from the mare until the gate was closed behind her.

"73," Mrs Troughton hollered.

"Yes, Ma'am," Johnny replied.

"Good luck, Mr Joe," Mrs. Troughton nodded. "That's a nice gelding you have."

"Thank you, Ma'am." Johnny tipped his hat to her too.

The crowd cheered as the Appaloosa left the ring and Johnny entered.

"Rider 73, Johnny Joe, riding Charlie Horse," the overhead speakers crackled.

Hannah stood in her stirrups so she could see over the gate.

Charlie Horse snorted and dug his hooves deep into the sand as Johnny let him canter up and down in front of the Starting Line for a moment. The big gelding's muscles rippled, and he arched his head down into his chest. The foghorn blew for the rider to proceed and Johnny put his heels to the tall Quarter Horse.

The gelding surged forward, leaving a deep rut in his wake. Johnny rounded the first barrel, letting the horse judge his own pace, then crossed over and took the second barrel. Charlie took the turn too sharply and Johnny's elbow hit the top of the barrel; it rocked, but stayed up. The crowd "oohed" and cheered. He flipped the reins over his leg and urged Charlie on. The big bay stretched out and ran. Johnny lifted the reins as he approached the last barrel in the cloverleaf, but Charlie turned wide. They skidded and slipped round the barrel, then headed for home. Charlie stretched his muscles and turned on the speed. The buzzer rang as Johnny and Charlie slid to a stop across the Finish Line.

"19.7 is now the time to beat," the speaker announced.

The crowd erupted. Last year's winning time was 20.5. Johnny had beaten the record.

"Yeeha!" Hannah cried. "Alright, Johnny."

Ross trotted Pizzazz up beside Hannah, Linda and Betty running along beside her.

"Did we just miss Johnny's ride?" he asked, breathlessly.

"Yes, you did. He rode a 19.7," Hannah beamed.

"Wow!" Linda said. "We're gonna grab a seat in the stands so we can cheer you guys on. We're late because we had to show Jenny where to go. She's sitting on Sal over by the out-gate." Linda pointed across the ring. Jenny waved from the other side, a wide grin on her face as she sat atop the purple-haired pony.

"This is really cool, Hannah," Betty added. "I'm definitely coming back next year. I'm gonna ask Mrs Troughton if I can ride Jiminy in it."

"76," Mrs. Troughton shouted over the babble.

"That's you, Hannah," Linda said, jumping up and down.

"You go, girl!" Betty raised her hands and gave Hannah a two thumbs up.

The girls giggled and ran to the stands. They jostled their way up several rows and plunked themselves down beside Hannah's mother and father. Mr and Mrs Joe sat on the other side of her parents. They all waved to her. Hannah noticed her mother looked a bit pale and that her father was sitting with his arm around her waist.

"Good luck, Hannah." Ross smiled. "Take some deep breaths and let Frosty do his thing. When you get to the end of your run, rein him to the right so that you don't slam into the fence. Frosty can't stop as short as Charlie or Pizzazz. Okay?"

"Okay," Hannah gasped, her hands visibly trembling.

Mrs Troughton opened the gate and Frosty pranced by her.

"Careful with that pony, Miss Storey. He's wilder than I've ever seen him," Mrs Troughton said, her eyebrows raised, worry lines etched into her forehead. "Are you sure about this?"

"We're okay, thank-you," Hannah tightened her grip on the reins as Frosty spooked sideways into the ring. Hannah took a couple of deep breaths and stroked his sweaty neck. Frosty danced in place. She realized that she must be as white as her mother if everyone kept asking her if she was okay.

"Easy boy," Hannah whispered to the gelding.

"Go, Hannah! Go, Frosty, go!" Linda and Betty screamed from the stands.

"Rider number 76. Hannah Storey and Mr Frost!" the loud speakers boomed.

The crowd erupted as Hannah lined Frosty up at the Starting Line. A chorus of "Go, Frosty! Go, Frosty! Go, Frosty, go!" thundered through the fairgrounds.

Hannah blushed and waved at the crowd, realizing that her misadventures had made her and Frosty famous.

"Oh, Lord. I hope we don't embarrass ourselves, Frosty," she muttered. Frosty stopped moving, swung his head around and playfully nipped Hannah's boot. He snorted and let out a little buck, then waited for Hannah's command. Hannah chuckled.

"Here we go," she said, grabbing hold of the saddle horn and squeezing her legs together.

Frosty reared and leapt forward, his muscles rippling. Hannah almost rolled off the back of the saddle, but snatched a handful of mane and managed to regain her balance. She heard the crowd rise to its feet, screaming and clapping wildly.

Hannah closed her legs around the gelding's barrel, leaned into the wind, and reined him toward the first barrel. Frosty's hooves dug deep, sand spitting out behind him, as he wheeled around the barrel. Hannah's knuckles turned white so she let go of the fistful of mane and switched one hand to the saddle horn. She lifted the reins with her left hand and pointed Frosty at the second bar-

76

rel. Her eyes watered. She wasn't prepared for the little mustang's speed.

The second barrel was gone in a blur as Hannah crossed over her path, gave Frosty his head and headed for the last barrel. The mustang snorted and plunged forward. Hannah felt like she had been strapped to a bolt of white lightning. A surge of sheer terror ripped through her chest. How was she going to stop? She had a vision of a shiny chrome grille and a big white truck skidding towards her and she screamed.

A roaring sound filled her ears; a tidal wave of shouts. She heard hundreds of people calling out her name. The little white gelding galloping beneath her spun around the third barrel like it wasn't there and headed for home.

Hannah grabbed hold of the saddle horn with both hands and hung on to it with all her strength. A white fence loomed up in front of her face. She leaned to the left and reined Frosty in. He swerved in response. Hannah's right leg slammed into the fence post as Frosty dug a trench alongside the fence, then skipped sideways, still at a gallop. Mrs Troughton clambered over the in-gate, her arms raised to slow the pony down, her eyes wide and frightened.

"Ladies and gentlemen, we have another new record," Pastor Smith's voice boomed over the fairground's speakers.

Hannah and Frosty blew past a startled Mrs Troughton. Hannah let go of the horn and slowly reined Frosty into a canter. They completed a lap around the ring. The people in the stands clapped. Frosty tipped his head to his chest as if acknowledging their cheers, his neck soaked with sweat, his nostrils flared and his tail held high in the air.

"18.5 is now the time to beat!" the loudspeaker crackled.

People screamed and stamped their feet.

Hannah grinned, wiped the sweat from her face and trotted Frosty to the exit gate.

Johnny was waiting for her, hat in hand, Charlie Horse resting his head on Johnny's shoulder.

"That was really something to see, Hannah," Johnny said, his eyes wide.

"Oh my God, Hannah. That was frightening. I'm sticking to jumping, I think it's safer," Jenny added, still perched atop Sal. Sal reached over and nuzzled Frosty as if to say, 'Good job, boyo!'.

"I can't believe it either. I've never been so scared in all my life," Hannah replied, jumping off of Frosty's back. "I hope my mother hasn't had a heart attack."

Johnny grabbed a hold of Frosty's reins. The gelding snorted, then nuzzled Johnny's hand gently.

"My legs are shaking, or at least the left one is," Hannah said, nervously. "I didn't think Frosty was going to stop. That was the longest 18 seconds in my life."

"Hannah, awesome!" Linda yelled as she and Betty came blasting around the corner. "No way can Ross and Pizzazz beat you. You were flying!"

Hannah laughed and stroked her pony's neck.

"Did you hear the crowd cheering for you and Frosty?" Betty asked, excitedly.

"Yeah. I think the whole world did," Hannah offered.

Johnny laughed.

"There goes Ross and Pizzazz," Jenny yelled. "Go, Ross!"

The kids turned and watched Ross and Pizzazz give it their best. A grey whirlwind, Pizzazz dug deep ruts around each barrel, but went wide on the last one, just like Charlie Horse did. The mare galloped, mane and tail flying, muscles rippling, then slid to a stop across the finish.

"Ladies and gentlemen, what a day we have here. Records are being broken at every turn. In Second Place, at 19 seconds even, we have Ross McCloud and Pizzazz. Hannah Storey and Mr Frost are still the time to beat at 18.5," Pastor Smith roared.

Ross trotted Pizzazz out of the ring.

"Nice job, Hannah," he said, then grinned.

"You too, Ross," Hannah replied. "You almost had us."

Ross laughed and dismounted Pizzazz. She was still blowing strong, her sides heaving. He patted her neck. "She gave it her best, but Frosty had wings."

"He did, and he scared the pants off me. I'm not going to do this again," Hannah confessed and gave Frosty a big hug.

"I'll ride him," Linda piped up.

"I don't think so," Ross answered, wagging a finger in her direction. He winked at Jenny. "You look good on that mare, Jen."

Jenny reached over and swatted Ross playfully on the arm.

"I feel like a granny in her rocker on this mare; she's like sitting on a couch. I'm so used to being much higher up. Pride is 17 hands. I almost couldn't see over the gate."

"Let's get these horses cooled off and tucked away," Johnny said. "There are still lots of competitors in our class, and we have to go carve our pumpkins for The Great Pumpkin Ride as well."

"And I still want to walk the maze," Hannah added.

"We'll help with the horses," Betty volunteered.

"Should we tell them now?" Linda giggled, elbowing Betty in the side.

Betty giggled. "I don't know. We might get into trouble."

Linda snorted.

"Tell us what?" Ross eyed his little sister suspiciously as they wandered in a group towards the back of the fairgrounds where makeshift stables had been fashioned for the horses.

"Welllll," Linda started.

Betty burst out laughing, hiccuped and snorted, gasping for breath.

Jenny leapt off Sal. She slapped Betty on the back a couple of times which sent Linda into a fit of stomach-grabbing giggles.

"Linda. What have you done?" Ross commanded.

"We kinda let the air out of Penny's tractor's tires," Linda confessed, her shoulders hunched over, a sheepish look on her face.

"I was the look-out," Betty offered, then started to giggle again.

"Oh, no. Penny's going to be furious!" Hannah gasped.

"You...You two...," Ross stammered.

"She missed her class and they wouldn't hold it because there are tons of entries in the Tractor Pull too!"

Linda quipped, straightening up and staring her big brother straight in the eye. What was done was done and Linda wasn't going to apologize for it. Linda figured it was pretty tame, all things considered.

"She was so mad, I thought her eyes were gonna pop out of her head and she was gonna explode like one of those cartoon characters," Betty added.

Linda and Betty looked at each other and started laughing again.

"Who is Penny?" Jenny asked.

Ross sighed and shook his head. "It's a long story; I'll fill you in while we're carving our pumpkins."

"You realize that Penny is gonna get seriously even with all of us?" Johnny glared at Linda and Betty, a worried Hannah biting her lip at his side.

Linda shrugged. "It was worth it," she said, defiantly.

"If anyone saw you, you and I will be grounded forever," Ross cautioned.

"There were so many people around that no one was paying attention to us. I just made out like it was my tractor and I was supposed to be there," Linda said.

"We waited for Penny to go to the biffy," Betty said, innocently.

"Remind me never to get on your bad side," Johnny ventured. He chuckled despite himself, then glanced at Hannah.

Hannah kept her opinions to herself and idly stroked Frosty's neck. She knew Penny would get them back. Penny didn't care who she hurt. She was the kid at school who liked to pull the legs off flies just for the fun of it.

Hannah knew that Penny wouldn't take this lightly. Linda and Betty had no idea what they had done.

"I don't want either of you to ever do anything like this again...okay?" Ross said quietly to Linda and Betty.

"We don't have to. She missed her class!" Linda said, innocently.

Ross laughed, despite himself.

"I mean it!"

"Fine," Linda said.

"Alright," Betty added.

The kids wandered away, horses in tow. They searched the crowd, keeping a look-out for Penny Paddington's strapping, angry, red-faced and red-haired form, but didn't see her all day.

Suddenly, they came to an abrupt halt.

Ole Man Levy walked toward them, his bald head gleaming in the fall sunlight. He was cleanly shaven, dressed in a starched white shirt and neatly pressed black trousers. The kids were surprised to see a gold "Judge" pin on his lapel. He stopped some distance away from Hannah and her pony.

"That was some job yer did, young lady," he said, his face flushed with embarrassment. "It was a sight. I'm glad yer okay from that fall yer took." He nodded and faded back into the crowd.

"Wow," Linda huffed.

"I'll say," Ross mumbled.

"I heard that he was judging the sheep, but didn't believe it," Johnny said. "Guess he was."

Hannah was shaken. She couldn't believe the old man had stopped judging long enough to watch her and Frosty run the barrels.

"Let's just go and water the horses," she said.

Everywhere Hannah, Johnny and Ross went, they were patted on the shoulder, as were their horses. All three of them had broken the Barrel Racing record. Hannah won First, Ross won Second, but Sam's new gelding beat Johnny and Charlie Horse by 2/10th's of a second, so Johnny placed Fourth.

Ross sheepishly confessed to Jenny about his plans for camping out after the Pumpkin Ride and apologized for not being able to see her off when the ride got back to town. Jenny was fine with it. Ross liked her even more for not asking to join them or being mad at him for not telling her.

All in all, the kids agreed that this Harvest Feast was one of the best ever.

Chapter Six

The Great Pumpkin Ride

Disorder ruled!

People, horses, dogs, wagons, and tractors were all jumbled up together at the end of the fairgrounds. Children screamed with delight, their tummies filled to bursting with apple cobbler and pumpkin pie. They darted in and out amongst the wagons, ran circles around the tractors, and ducked underneath horses' legs to the not-so-polite shouts of the horsemen perched atop their steeds. The kids were lucky that most of the horses were already exhausted from the day's events and stood quietly watching the commotion around them.

Hannah sat astride Frosty, fidgeting with the top of the evil, slant-eyed pumpkin that sat wedged between her stomach and the saddle horn. Frosty snorted and pinned his ears back at the group of seven year old boys who dashed by him holding pumpkins on their heads and shouting, "Make way for the Headless Horsemen".

Johnny rested his pumpkin on his right hip and yelled at the group of kids, "Watch out for that Appaloosa mare up there or you will be headless horsemen!"

"Serve them right," Linda quipped from the far side of Johnny and Charlie Horse, poking a hole through the bottom of a pumpkin no bigger than an acorn squash. The pumpkin was the smallest one in the pile beside the pumpkin carving table. The reason for picking it was: "the orange clashes with Sal's purple hair", or so she had told Betty. With a sigh of satisfaction, Linda tied the tiny pumpkin to the thick bedroll on the back of her saddle; it leered at Hannah and Frosty, with its top askew.

"Is it true?" Betty asked, bouncing up to Linda and Sal.

"What?" Linda asked sheepishly.

"Are you guys really camping out at a haunted cabin tonight?"

"Who told you?" Linda sulked.

"Everyone's talking about it. How come you didn't tell me?" Betty warbled, tears in her eyes.

"Because it was a secret and I didn't know you when we planned it," Linda said, gently, hating the disappointment she saw in Betty's eyes. She didn't mean to hurt her new friend's feelings. "Jenny isn't coming either."

Betty sniffed. "Okay, but you will tell me all about it tomorrow, right?"

"Oh, yeah," Linda agreed.

"Aren't you afraid?" Betty asked, stroking the soft hairs on Sal's nuzzle. Sal sighed with delight.

"No way. Ross will look after me; he always does." Linda grinned.

"Will you ride behind the wagon that I'm in? I think Jenny and I are going to be in the same one. Mrs Troughton arranged it."

"You bet I will," Linda reached down and patted her friend on the shoulder. "Next year, we'll have our own camp-out. We can sleep in the hayloft in our barn."

"Cosmo," Betty said, her face brightening.

The girls giggled.

A cloud of thick black smoke filled the air like a grass fire on a still summer's night as a tractor rumbled by. It smothered the girls and made them gag. Penny Paddington's dad rolled past them driving his old John Deere with Penny sitting on one fender, her feet on the step and a dark look of hatred on her face.

Linda's mouth went dry. Betty sidled sideways and stood on Sal's far side, watching Penny go by from the safety of Sal's broad shoulder.

Penny grinned crookedly, then raised one hand and fired an imaginary shot at them with one finger.

The girls blanched. Penny knew!

Penny and her father made their way up the long line of riders and wagons to the head of the gathering as Hannah, Johnny, Linda and Betty watched nervously. Mr Paddington was the Grand Master of The Great Pumpkin Ride so they were going to have to endure Penny's wrath all the way to Pumpkin Alley. Ross hadn't seen her; his hands were full helping Mr Storey and Jenny load the huge pumpkin she had carved into the back of one of the wagons.

"Don't let her scare you, girls," Johnny leaned over Charlie's neck and patted Betty on the shoulder. "It'll just spoil the Pumpkin Ride."

86

"Johnny's right. Ignore her," Hannah spoke quietly. She turned in her saddle and smiled at Johnny. "What about you? Are you still okay with this tonight?"

Johnny nodded and smiled back.

"Listen up, folks. The Grand Master of The Great Pumpkin Ride has signaled that we're ready. Horse-drawn carriages first, followed by horse drawn wagons and tractors with wagons at the back. You folks on horses can ride in groups or with the wagons. Make sure you have matches or lighters in your pocket. Signal if you don't and someone'll help you out. Keep the little ones close; we don't want to lose any of 'em. Wagons Ho!" Pastor Smith yelled over the heads of the crowd, his voice hoarse from the long day of announcing. He was greeted by a chorus of cheers.

KABANG!

The starting gun went off. Horses snorted and danced, sloughing off their tiredness. Mr Paddington revved up his tractor and started down the winding trail. The tractor settled into a slow, rambling pace, its low rumbling purr sounding like an asthmatic cat getting its chin rubbed.

Every wagon was filled to overflowing with people holding pumpkins. There were great peels of laughter and endless chatter up and down the wagon train. Little ones swayed in their mother's laps; babies slept in their grandmother's arms; father's rode beside or behind wagons, sons and daughters at their side. Each rider had a carved-out pumpkin on their lap or fastened to their saddle horn. There were baby pumpkins like Linda's and ordinary pumpkins the size of beach balls, plus two gigantic ones which took up the whole back of the

Albertson's wagon. One of the giant pumpkins had a wizard carved into its flesh with a dragon at his heels; the other was painted like a clown with white smiling lips, rosy red cheeks and a Delicious apple for its nose.

For almost a mile, the riders and wagons stretched out from the fairground, through the fields, and along the trail atop the high gravelly banks of the Athabasca River. The horizon was scarlet, the sun just beginning to set over the tilled fields across the river. The North Star twinkled brightly overhead and a sliver of moon rose gracefully over the treetops as the sun disappeared completely. A fine mist rose off the river and drifted over the line of people and horses, the dew drops thickening and gathering together in a ghostly fog that hushed the most unruly teen. The Great Pumpkin Ride had officially begun and the river had christened its beginning once again.

Hannah shivered. She zipped up her jacket and hunched down in her saddle. Her long black hair glistened, bejewelled like a spider's web in the morning. The fog steadily rolled over the wagon train in an ever-thickening cloud.

The chitter-chatter stopped. No one laughed, but it wasn't silent. The air was filled with a concert of sounds from the jingle of harness, the squeak of leather, the clip clop of horses hooves, the low purr of a few tractors, to the water gurgling over rocks in the riverbed below.

Hannah stole a cautious glance over the bank. The river was as black and endless as a newly dug grave. Hannah wouldn't have been surprised to see those ghostly fishermen climbing up the banks in their red-checked shirts and green hip-waders, their face white and swollen, their eyes hollow as death. She turned her head aside and thought she saw a tiny raven-haired woman walking beside her, a playful smile on her lips, a tartan draped over her shoulders, and a little jig in every step.

Hannah gasped!

Was that her Gram?

Hannah blinked and the image was gone.

Johnny eased Charlie Horse up beside her. Hannah shook herself. She was letting her mind carry her away. How was she going to make it through the night if a wee bit of fog got her that spooked?

Johnny reached over and picked up her hand, holding it tightly in his own. The warmth of his firm and calloused grip made Hannah feel better. She smiled up at him. Johnny smiled back.

Linda and Ross rode in front of them. Betty and Jenny sat together in the back of the wagon directly ahead of the McClouds, holding hands and dangling their legs over the side. Betty continuously looked from side to side, clearly shaken by the cold, dark night that surrounded her.

Hannah swivelled in the saddle and looked at the riders behind her. Many of them were holding hands, staving off the chill and comforting each other. Hannah was relieved to see it. She stood up in her stirrups and looked over Jenny's head, her mother and father were holding hands too.

The sky seemed to fall down around the wagon train, closing in on it like the walls of a cave. Tiny flickering candle lights hovered in the air a dozen paces from the cliff top, dancing on the shroud of fog that covered the river valley, waiting for the Pumpkin Ride's return.

Lanterns were struck, hissing into life from the front and back of each wagon and tractor, but the forest ahead was so dense that the light from the lanterns couldn't penetrate it.

"Light the candle in your pumpkin," Johnny whispered to Hannah.

Hannah fumbled in her pocket, found the lighter her father had given her and flicked the lever with her thumb. The flame jumped into life. She lifted the top off her pumpkin and lit the candle inside.

Matches were struck. Pumpkins glowed and bobbed up and down the line of riders, stretching through the forest as far as the eye could see. Horses snorted nervously. Riders made shushing noises to try and settle them down.

Hannah's body was racked with shivers, and she chewed her upper lip raw. Frosty grunted from deep down in his chest, a hollow protest. Charlie Horse crowded in close to Frosty. Johnny's right leg rubbed against Hannah's left and she was grateful for the warmth it offered.

Linda turned around in her saddle and gave Hannah and Johnny a shaky salute. Johnny chuckled under his breath, his wide and amiable face glowing softly, basked by the golden warmth provided by his pumpkin.

"End of the line, folks," Mr Paddington shouted, breaking everyone's revery. There was a series of nervous chuckles. "I declare that Pumpkin Alley is open. Pick your trees and plant your pumpkins."

"This is it," Johnny said and swung his leg over Charlie's back. He walked around the gelding and helped Hannah off her mustang.

The spell was broken. People chatted and joked together. Weary horses breathed a sigh of relief. Children laughed. No one minded them getting underfoot.

All through the forest, the townsfolk laid their pumpkins to rest in select spots beside the trail, between the gnarly roots of trees, and on top of rotting, moss-covered stumps. Kids ran to and fro, darting in and out amongst the pumpkins. Families walked together and chatted amiably. The wranglers turned the wagons around and rolled by the townsfolk with a jingle of harness and a few well-placed shouts, getting ready for the trek home.

Mr Paddington drove his tractor by the kids. Penny wasn't standing on the back. They glanced nervously at each other.

"I swear she was standing on the back of that tractor all the way along the river," Ross muttered to Johnny.

"Yeah, I saw her too," Johnny replied.

Hannah looked up and down the line of wandering families, but didn't see Penny anywhere. She thought she saw Ole Man Levy in a thick winter jacket, his dirty old baseball cap tipped backwards on his head, place a pumpkin on a fallen log, but he was gone in a flash, just like the image of her Gram walking on the trail beside Frosty. She had a hard time believing that Ole Man Levy would join The Great Pumpkin Ride, but what did she know?

"That can't be good sign, Penny not being with her dad," she whispered.

Ross and Johnny shook their heads.

"I'm sure we just missed her. Look at all the people...all of River Bend and half of Cold River are out here," Johnny said, wisely.

"Yeah, I thought I just saw Ole Man Levy put a pumpkin down on that log over there," Hannah ventured, pointing off to her left.

"No way! This is the biggest Pumpkin Ride in River Bend's history," Ross finished.

Jenny and Betty skipped up alongside of Ross and Linda.

"This is just too cool," Betty said, hopping from one foot to the other. "Did you guys see those candle lights over the river? They were like hovering in the air over the cliff. What were they?"

"How does everyone see without their pumpkins on the way back? It is so dark out here," Jenny moved closer to Ross. "Betty's right. What were those lights?"

Ross grinned.

"There is a whole wagon full of lanterns that brings up the back of the ride. The Grand Master will bring the lanterns out in about half an hour after everyone has walked Pumpkin Alley," Johnny answered.

"I don't know what those candle lights are," Ross said. "Something weird like that happens every year. No one knows what causes it and no one has ever seen them except on the Pumpkin Ride."

"Well, I'm glad we'll all have lanterns on the way back. This forest gives me the creeps. I swear the trees keep moving in towards the road. It's like they're trying to walk right over us."

"You too?" Hannah looked at Jenny. "That's how this place makes me feel."

"Hannah calls Pumpkin Alley, 'Sleepy Hollow'," Ross added.

"I can see why," Jenny muttered, shrugging her shoulders and snuggling deeper into her own quilted coat. She pulled her woolen hat down low over her red ears.

The kids led their horses up and down Pumpkin Alley, wandering in and out of the pumpkins, discussing the merits of each one. None of them wanted to discuss the upcoming ride to the trapper's cabin. Linda's favorite was a dragon whose spiky tail wound deep within the pumpkin's orange flesh. Hannah loved the giant clown that had been placed at the end of the trail thanks to the efforts of four strong men. Jenny liked the giant wizard. Ross and Johnny couldn't decide on a favorite; they loved them all.

Mr and Mrs Joe found the kids huddled in a group at the end of the trail, staring off into the darkness, their horses at their side.

"Are we still gonna do it?" Ross asked, Jenny holding onto one arm and not looking very happy.

"It's a lot spookier than I thought it'd be," Linda admitted.

"I don't mind one way or the other. Johnny?" Hannah asked.

"I have to," Johnny spoke, his voice raw and trembling.

Mrs Joe nodded at her son. She was wrapped in a knee length felt coat with a red Coho Salmon stitched on the back, her breath a cold stream in front of her face. "I want you each to take one of these medicine bundles and wear it around your neck. They will protect you." She

93

smiled and handed a small leather bound packet with a beaded leather necklace to each of the kids, then kissed her son on the cheek. "You kids be careful in the dark. Don't worry about ghosts, just the things that you can't see on the trail. Spirits can guide you; they aren't all bad, remember that!"

"Listen to your mom, Johnny," Mr Joe added. "Take my cellular with you. If you get into trouble, call me or Ross and Linda's dad. We'll come out with the ATV's and get you kids. Promise?"

"We promise," the kids said in unison.

Mr and Mrs McCloud joined the group standing at the head of the trail. Mr McCloud had three lanterns in his hand. The lanterns banged together, casting a white glow and illuminating the mangled trees that crouched around the crowd of on-lookers that had heard about the kid's great adventure and had gathered to see them off.

"Get off the trail if you hear the Headless Horseman coming, you guys," Sam shouted from amidst the crowd of people.

"Watch out for bedbugs and things that go bump in the night," called Albert.

There were a series of half-hearted giggles; a couple of little ones broke into tears. It was clear that most of the folks on the Pumpkin Ride thought the small group of kids insane to go camping in the bush on Halloween night.

"Don't be too scared to phone us if you need anything at all, you hear?" Tom McCloud said as he handed one lantern each to Ross, Johnny and Hannah.

"Don't I get one?" Linda sulked.

"You stay right behind your brother at all times, young lady, and keep both hands on the reins," her father ordered.

Linda nodded, smart enough not to question her dad at this point, lest he pull her out of the camp-out.

"We'll be home for breakfast," Ross said, placing a foot in the stirrup and swinging into the saddle.

"We'll have eggs and bacon and bannock ready when you get home," Mrs Joe said.

Johnny smiled.

"Be careful, please," Jenny whispered to Ross, standing by his leg.

"I will," he whispered back, then wheeled Pizzazz to face the darkened trail before him. "Ready?"

"Ready," Johnny, Hannah and Linda answered, mounting their horses and following after Ross.

Linda rode directly behind her brother, as ordered, with Hannah and Johnny pulling up the rear. They turned and waved at their parents.

The trail they rode out on was a wall of darkness broken only by the thin beams of light cast by their lanterns. The comforting light coming from Pumpkin Alley, from the row on row of lit pumpkins and the Coleman lanterns fixed to the tractors and the wagons, was quickly swallowed up as the kids rounded the first bend in the trail that led to the cabin.

Far behind them they heard Sam and Albert singing the theme to "Ghostbusters": "When there's somethin' wrong, in your neighborhood...Who ya gonna call? Ghostbusters!"

"Who's afraid of those ghosts?" Sam screeched.

"I ain't afraid of no ghosts," Albert hollered.

The kids chuckled, boosted by the confidence of their friends.

Chapter Seven

All Hallow's Eve

A night owl hooted from the naked branches of a poplar tree off to the right of the trail. Linda jumped in her saddle. Sal snorted and spooked sideways. Linda lifted the reins and moved her little mare back behind her brother and Pizzazz, so close that Sal's nose touched Pizzazz' tail. For once, Pizzazz didn't seem to mind.

The light cast from the three lanterns bobbed along the ground, creating long shadows of the horses' legs. The glow was unable to penetrate the darkness on the opposite side of the horse on which it was carried. The stark whiteness of the light caused the trees beside the trail to look feeble and scabrous, as if they had been infected with leprosy.

The night sky overhead was an endless blanket of twinkling stars, now visible because the canopy of evergreens that bordered Pumpkin Alley was far behind the lonely group of riders. The poplar stand that stood sentinel on either side of the trail was leafless, the trees pre-

97

pared for an early winter, a quarter moon hanging low in the sky just out of reach of their skeletal arms. A light layer of fog rose from the leaf strewn ground as if the earth itself was alive and breathing quietly in its sleep.

Several pale, flickering lights skipped through the shadows in the forest, matching the pace of the four steeds. The lights were like gossamer threads, thin and reedy. They were accompanied by a soft clip clopping sound that echoed through the darkness like the last note of a flute, held in place until the flutist ran out of air.

"Did you see that? Did you see those lights?" Linda whispered urgently.

"What?" Ross asked, his voice sharp. His nerves were frayed.

"I did," Hannah responded, shakily. "They aren't like the candle lights over the river, they're more like wisps of cloud, drifting amidst the trees."

"I think it's ground fog. It was hot this afternoon and the temperature's really dropped since then. It's gotta be the light from the lanterns bouncing off pockets of fog," offered Ross.

The kids reined in their horses. All four horses and kids turned to look into the bush. The horses' ears were pricked forward, listening, the hairs on their necks quivering. Pizzazz blew a note of warning and swished her tail dangerously. Frosty let out a low nicker. The rhythmic beat of hoof falls abruptly stopped.

The bush rattled and the ghost lights flickered through the trees, passing them by. Pizzazz blew wind.

"Whoa, girl," Ross said, quietly. "Come on, let's hurry and get to the cabin. A fire will chase away these spooks."

"Good idea," Hannah said. "My hands and toes are frozen."

"You okay, Lindy?" Ross asked.

"I guess, but I don't see how that ground fog of yours can sound like a cavalry of horses walking by," Linda squeaked.

Ross squeezed his legs against his mare's sides and she stepped forward, hesitating once, then doing as commanded. The others followed close behind, their horses walking nose to tail.

They quickly caught up with the bobbing white lights, flickering grey shadows that danced between the trees. The ghost lights had elongated and were more solid, not appearing as lights anymore, but smokey figures on horseback. The ghostly riders were featureless, a vision lost if one looked too closely. They stretched back several paces from the group of teens.

Clip, drop, clop. Clip, drop, clop.

The hoof beats sounded like a leaky water faucet. The horses responded with nervous whinnies and a quickening in their steps.

"Rossss," Linda wailed under her breath.

"Ignore it, Lindy. There's nothing there," commanded her brother.

"How far to the cabin?" Hannah asked through chattering teeth, glancing nervously over her shoulder at Johnny. He rode stiff-shouldered, his face rigid and his eyes gazing off into the distance.

"Five minutes or so," Ross answered.

The kids scanned the bush for whatever or whoever was keeping pace with them, their grip on their nerves fragile and their minds a heartbeat away from total panic.

All at once, the ghost lights disappeared. The sounds of the forest returned to normal.

A whippoorwill let out a lonely call; a grey owl hooted in response.

With a weary sigh, the riders broke through the thicket that marked the end of the trail and emerged on the clearing that bordered the cabin. A light breeze whispered to the night, gently ruffling the horses' manes and the girls' hair.

A low, hoarse chuckle rippled through the air. The bushes to their left rattled, the last of the dead leaves fluttering to the ground.

Charlie Horse reared and danced sideways, slamming Johnny's arm into a tree. The Quarter Horse was still ruffled from the ride in.

"Did you hear that?" Johnny said, his voice calm and steady. "We have company, I think."

"What kind of company?" Linda asked, her eyes wide with terror. "I don't want to see anymore ghost lights."

"Two-legged, I believe," Johnny replied.

"I hope so," Hannah muttered.

Ross trotted across the glade and up to the cabin, then dismounted quickly.

"Forget the noises! Let's get a big fire going, then we'll see what we can see," Ross added, nodding at Johnny as he reined Charlie Horse in beside Pizzazz.

Four shadows capered across the mossy log walls of the cabin as the kids placed the lanterns on the porch and quickly un-tacked their mounts. Hannah helped Linda with Sal. Linda's bravery had all but disappeared with the ghost lights that followed them from Pumpkin Alley.

Linda was suddenly just a scared ten year old kid. Hannah was quite shaken too, but helping Linda kept her mind off her own fears.

"I'm guessing that we're thinking the same way," Ross whispered to Johnny, out of the girls' earshot.

"The Phantom Menace?" Johnny added, grinning sideways at Ross as he undid his cinch and slipped the saddle off his gelding.

"Yeah. A big red devil," Ross returned.

"Let's get the fire going and see if we can flush her out."

Ross nodded in agreement.

The boys placed their saddles on the porch and went into the cabin to retrieve some of the firewood and kindling they had stored inside after they had finished making the corral. They'd had a feeling it was going to be wet and wanted to be prepared.

Johnny formed a steeple of kindling and lit the mound of dry branches. The kindling burst into flame. Slowly, he added the larger branches that Ross handed him until the fire was good and hot.

The girls untied all the bedrolls from the back of the saddles and placed them in a stack beside the fire pit. Hannah shook out a blanket and wrapped it around her shoulders. She had never felt so cold in all her life. Her teeth slowly stopped chattering as the heat from the fire and the woolen blanket finally warmed up her hands and face.

"We'll take the horses around the back if you girls want to warm up?" Ross offered.

"For once, I won't argue with you, big brother," Linda said. "I'm not leaving here."

Johnny and Ross gathered up the horses, but Sal refused to be led away from the warmth of the fire. She stood solidly in place, halfway between the cabin's porch and the fire pit, head in the air, refusing to be dragged, prodded, or clucked forward. Frosty seemed to agree with her and danced backwards on the lead line, his tail falling dangerously close to the flames.

Hannah ran forward and tugged Frosty's lead rope out of Johnny's hand.

"Well I guess Frosty's cold too," Johnny ventured, shaking his head.

"They won't go anywhere...they didn't before," Hannah said, gently stroking Frosty's neck. He lowered his head and snuggled up to his master. Hannah chuckled.

"Probably not," Ross agreed. "All that work building the corral for nothing. Go figure. Who'd have thought the horses would be afraid of ghosts too?"

"No more ghosts!" Linda said, defiant. "I don't want to think anymore about those lights in the forest."

"That was just swamp gas and imagination. I'm sure of it," Ross answered. "Don't you think so, Johnny?"

"Sounds fine to me," Johnny agreed, looking down at his feet. He banged a toe against one of the fire pit rocks.

"Yeah, right, swamp gas," Linda eyeballed her brother.

Johnny looked up and burst out laughing. Linda slapped her brother in the arm and started giggling too.

"Let's get our bedrolls out and sit by the fire. I'm just going to let Frosty go with his halter on. I know he'll stay close." Hannah led Frosty away from the fire, un-clipped the lead line and gave him a final pat. She walked back to her gear and snatched up her sleeping bag and blue plastic ground sheet, not noticing that Frosty had followed along behind her like a lost puppy. The gelding stopped and sighed contentedly when he found a few blades of grass to nibble on a few feet from where Hannah was shaking out her bedroll.

Johnny watched Frosty graze, each bite taking him closer and closer to Hannah while she snuggled down inside her sleeping bag, oblivious to his movements. Johnny grinned and let Charlie Horse go, then prepared his own bed.

Linda and Ross did the same. They placed a plastic sheet on the ground to keep them dry, then their sleeping bags over top.

"Look at the horses," Linda said, glancing over her shoulder to where Sal grazed peacefully beside Frosty, Charlie and Pizzazz on either side. The horses had formed a semi- circle at the teens' backs, all of them just a few short paces away. "It's almost like they're protecting us, isn't it?"

"Yeah," Ross ventured. "Weird."

"Cosmo," Linda said, under her breath.

"Very cosmo," Hannah added.

"Betty's gonna love it when I tell her about this. She sure fell in love with Sal."

Linda leaned her head against her saddle, her pillow for the night, and looked at the stars as she snuggled deep inside her sleeping bag to get warm. Her face was red from the cold and her breath a frothy steam in front of her face. "Have you ever seen so many stars in all your life?" she asked breathlessly.

"Sure is beautiful. You don't see this in the city; there are too many lights," Hannah responded. She leaned on one elbow and looked up at the starry canopy overhead. The night was crystal clear. The moon looked like it had been painted on the heavens, it was so crisp and bright.

The fire snapped and crackled as pockets of sap exploded into flames.

Get out! You're not wanted here!

The kids mouths dropped open and their eyebrows raised. The horses lifted their heads and looked over top of the crackling fire into the forest.

It came again. A soft whisper, faint as the evening's breeze.

Get out! You're not wanted here!

"Rossss," Linda cried out.

"Hey, who is it? Who's there?" Ross shouted.

"That's enough, Penny," yelled Johnny. "We know it's you. Come on out'a there."

Pizzazz stamped a foot angrily behind him.

Get out! You're not wanted here!

Louder the whispering came.

"Ross, I'm scared," Linda muttered, tears in her eyes.

Hannah reached out and drew Linda close to her.

Bang! Rat-ta-tat-tat!

The bushes around the cabin exploded in a flurry of sparks. Pizzazz reared, screamed and bolted across the clearing. Sal bucked and trotted after her. Frosty reared and pawed the earth, Charlie Horse stamping the ground angrily at his side.

"Sal!" Linda screamed. "Don't leave me!"

104

Sal skidded to a stop and wheeled on her haunches. She trotted furiously back to Linda, her eyes rolling in terror.

"Pizzazz," Ross roared.

"Whoa, fellas," Johnny said, leaping to his feet and grabbing hold of Frosty's and Charlie's halters. The geldings snorted, but stood their ground.

"Ha, ha, ha!" a red-faced Penny Paddington laughed as she emerged from the bushes. "Got ya good."

She capered around the side of the cabin like a ghoul, a wicked grin on her face, her eyes glowing in the light cast by the dancing fire.

"Bet you won't ever see that mare again. Nananananah...," she howled.

"You bag!" Ross yelled.

"That'll teach you to keep that little brat sister of yours away from me and mine," Penny squealed, still dancing around and around in a jig. She stopped. "What did ya expect? I had to finish off those firecrackers somewhere."

"That was really cruel, Penny," Hannah replied, Linda sniffling in misery beside her.

Sal walked over and tucked her head protectively over Linda's thin shoulders, pulling her in close to her chest as if to say, "I'm with you, buddy."

"That's it," Ross wailed and ran towards Penny.

Penny dodged Ross' tackle and ran into the bush. Ross landed in a heap in the dirt. Penny laughed uproariously.

BANG!

Brrrrruuummmmm!

The bushes burst open. Penny careened through them on her yellow Honda motorbike, tearing the roots out with the chain. She skidded the bike around in a tight circle, spraying Ross with a wave of gravel and dirt.

"Owwww," he howled like a scalded cat.

Penny doubled over with laughter, then gunned the bike and slapped it into gear. She skipped across the clearing, the motorbike's tires bouncing off rocks, its headlight disappearing up the trail.

Ross stood up and brushed himself off.

"That witch!" he growled.

"Are you hurt?" Hannah asked, descending on Ross to make sure he wasn't bleeding anywhere.

"I'm fine," he muttered.

"That was really stupid, not that Penny's that bright anyway," Johnny added. "Don't worry about your mare. Pizzazz'll either find her way home or her way back here."

"Yeah, I guess, but if she doesn't come back, I'll have to pack her saddle home myself," Ross sulked.

Linda giggled, thinking of the looks on her parent's faces when her brother walked up the lane, his face tired and dripping with sweat, Pizzazz' saddle draped over one shoulder.

"That's not funny, Linda. I know what you're thinking," he said.

"Yeah, it really would be, bro," Linda said.

Hannah chuckled, then burst out laughing. The boys quickly joined in.

"Do you think I should phone my dad and tell him not to worry?" Ross asked Johnny once he had finished laughing.

"No. He'll see that Pizzazz has a halter on and figure she broke out of our corral," Johnny replied. "Pizzazz does have a reputation to uphold."

Ross roared with laughter, his anger spent.

"She sure does. I guess we know where those lights in the forest came from."

"Yeah, I guess," Johnny nodded.

"I don't think so..." Hannah said, her voice trailing off.

"Why's that?" Ross asked.

"If Penny made all those lights and noises, then how come I heard horses! I'm sure I saw riders too! Penny rides a motorbike because she doesn't own a horse!" Hannah glanced from Ross to Johnny. The boys shrugged, neither having an answer.

"Who's afraid of those ghosts?" Linda singsonged. "I ain't afraid of no ghosts."

Ross gave his sister a quick one-armed hug.

"Neither am I. It's too cold to go chasing after ghosts or that silly mare of mine," Ross declared.

The kids threw a few more logs on the burning coals, wanting to make the fire as big as possible, and snuggled down inside their sleeping bags once again. They talked quietly, but decided not to tell any ghost stories. The Great Pumpkin Ride and the trip to the cabin was scary enough. They all agreed that this was the spookiest Halloween ever. Linda was back to her chatty little self, lifting the spirits of her brother and her friends. The fire crackled and lulled them into a calm peacefulness.

A fine layer of dew soaked the dried grasses outside the fire's circle. The stars above glittered and twinkled. A

107

satellite passed overhead, a red and white winking light that streaked across the horizon.

Linda handed around a canteen of iced tea. Ross pulled a bag of Cheezies from his pack, made a little orange pile in his lap, then passed the bag to Linda.

"I can't believe I forgot the marshmallows," Hannah groaned.

"I don't think we really need any." Johnny offered, "Mom gave me a packet of smoked salmon and some pemmican if any of you want some. It's in my saddle bag. I'm so full from that slab of barbequed beef I ate at dinner that I heard Charlie Horse groan when I put a foot in the stirrup."

"You forgot the part afterwards," Hannah teased.

Johnny raised an eyebrow.

"You know, the slice of apple pie and the slice of pumpkin pie that followed that," she finished.

"And Mom tells me that I can pack it away," Ross added, then chuckled deeply.

Johnny smiled and shrugged his shoulders.

"I wouldn't mind some of that smoked salmon later, but....well...I know you all don't mind, but...," Hannah stammered, really uncomfortable by what she was going to have to ask.

"But what?" Linda asked, her head tilted to one side.

Hannah gulped. "I have to take my leg off to sleep."

"Geez, I never thought about that," Ross said.

"It's okay, Hannah. We don't care. You should know that," Linda squeaked, then giggled. "Can I see it?"

Hannah laughed, her voice a little shaky.

"Yeah, you can see it. I guess you all will."

108

Hannah unzipped her sleeping bag and rolled up the right leg of her jeans. Her riding boots were already set neatly by the fire at the foot of her sleeping bag, toes to the flames, so that they would stay warm and dry for the morning. She pulled up her white cotton longjohns and exposed the top of her prosthetic leg. She could feel her face turning red. She had never removed her leg in front of anyone except for her parents and her doctor. She wondered if her friends would treat her any differently after this.

"Cool," Ross said, leaning over his sister's shoulder so that he could see it too!

"There's nothing cool about it," Hannah replied stiffly.

Johnny placed a hand on her shoulder and squeezed gently. Hannah smiled, but her eyes remained distant and cold as she tugged on the prosthetic leg. It came off with a light sucking sound. Her stump was red and calloused. She reached down and massaged some life back into the skin. It had been a long day with very little rest.

At the sight of the stump, so raw and painful looking, none of the kids had anything to say, not even Linda. They watched Hannah reach inside her pack, pull out some liniment and massage it into the stump with a faint sigh of relief.

Hannah glanced sideways at Johnny and was thankful to see a slow, lazy smile return to his face. He hadn't smiled much for several days, not since last weekend when they found the Medicine Wheel. Hannah was glad to see the smile, but happier to see that he didn't flinch at the sight of her missing limb.

109

Hannah finished her chores, then pulled the sleeping bag back around her and zipped it up. She propped her prosthetic against the saddle and threw a towel over it to keep it from getting too damp.

"That hurts a lot, doesn't it?" Linda asked, filled with curiosity.

Ross grunted a warning, but his little sister ignored him.

"Sometimes. Mostly on long days like today." Hannah smiled. "I'm used to it. You just have to deal with it. I can't change anything."

The gang settled back and relaxed with Frosty, Sal and Charlie Horse close to their backs. The horses seemed to enjoy the camaraderie around the fire.

The evening drifted on, hour by hour. The fog in the meadow grew thicker and swirled around the horses legs. It tugged at the campfire's edges. The kids grew sleepy and dozed inside their sleeping bags, their heads resting on their saddles.

The cabin behind them started to smoulder inside with an un-earthly fire, yet the house was empty, void of warmth and comfort. The world ended a few feet past the tree line. The grey stones of the Medicine Wheel shifted in shape, bending over the stalks of yellowed grass in the meadow and smoothing them under as they grew and shrank with a rhythm all their own. Several stones pulsed with a savage life, a light so harsh it was like a lightning bolt splitting the heavens in half on a humid August night.

The throbbing white heat cast from the Medicine Wheel burned Johnny's eyelids. He opened his eyes and

110

looked at the stones. He idly watched them shrink and grow, thinking that he was dreaming.

The Medicine Wheel's edges grew more refined, the rocks brighter, shifting and changing from a dull grey to a golden yellow. With each shift, pebble to boulder, the rocks in the Wheel began to hum, a low vibration that sounded like someone had blown on a piece of paper wrapped around a comb. The humming grew steadily louder. Startled, Johnny bolted upright in his sleeping bag, then quickly stood up, his eyes fixed on the pulsating stones of the Medicine Wheel.

The others woke and sat up, startled by Johnny's rising. They were unable to hear the storm that was building inside Johnny's head, and they cast worried looks at each other. Was it a nightmare? Why were Johnny's shoulders shaking and why was his head bobbing from side to side?

"Johnny?" Hannah questioned, her voice dry and raspy.

Johnny didn't answer. He continued to stand, his swaying growing more violent, his eyes fixed on the center of the clearing. His face was pale, all traces of his earlier smile were gone.

"Hey, pal, what's up? The Boogeyman got your tongue?" Ross' words drifted away, the joke falling flat.

Linda sidled over closer to Hannah. Ross unzipped his sleeping bag and knelt down beside Linda, guarding his sister's back.

Dum, tom, tom.

The drumming sounded faint at first as if it came from deep within the earth. Before long, it had grown into waves of pulsating sounds that vibrated through every nerve and cell. Hannah clenched her teeth, her ears hurting.

Dum, tom, tom. Dum, tom, tom. Dum, tom, tom.

The stones of the Medicine Wheel throbbed with ghastly shades of bright orange. Tendrils of mist rose in a ghostly stream out of each stone as if the stone was giving birth to it. The columns of mist swirled and swayed, then broke free of the stone that birthed it and danced along the ground, hopping from rock to rock of its own free will. The night was calm and still with no wind to carry the mists forward.

The horses continued to stand, heads down and snoozing several paces from the fire pit, not bothered by the sound of the drums nor the brightness of the once sleepy meadow.

Johnny reached down and tugged on his boots. He walked around the fire and stood looking into the center of the Medicine Wheel, the campfire's flames a dull glow at his back. His toe started to move within his boot; slightly, ever so slightly, as if it had a will of its own. Every fibre of Johnny's being wanted to reach out to the tendrils of mist that gathered in the middle of the clearing and join the ballet.

"Come...Dance...Dance with us," the mist whispered and swayed.

Johnny knew his time had come; it was time to dance.

Chapter Eight

The Fiddle and The Drum

"Johnny? Stop it, please," Hannah pleaded.

Johnny stopped swaying back and forth, and stood motionless for a moment, but didn't turn around.

Hannah unzipped her sleeping bag, tossed the towel off her prosthetic leg and fumbled with the prosthetic, trying to get it in position, but the toe kept getting caught on the inside of her sleeping bag. She pulled up her right pant leg and slammed her stump down hard into the molded socket. The pain was horrific. She winced and quickly pulled on her boots, then hobbled around the fire.

"Hannah, wait!" Ross ordered, but Hannah didn't heed him. "Get your boots on, Lindy."

Ross and Linda donned their jackets and boots and ran after Hannah.

"It's like he's in a trance," Hannah said, waving a hand in front of Johnny's blank face. His eyelids didn't even blink.

"Johnny!" Ross shouted in his ear. Still, no response.

Ross grabbed him by the shoulders and shook him violently. Johnny groaned. His eyes fluttered, the pupils beginning to focus. Ross gave him another quick shake. "Come on, Johnny, snap out of it. You're sleep walkin', buddy."

"You guys," Linda stammered.

"What?" Ross asked, standing in front of Johnny, his back to the clearing.

"Look!" Linda said in awe.

Annoyed, Ross glanced over his shoulder.

"Oh, wow!" he exclaimed, spinning on his heel and turning a deathly shade of white.

A huge, unearthly teepee of flame reached upwards from the center of the Medicine Wheel. It was a fire without logs, composed only of flames, blue at the base and bright yellow as it stretched high into the night sky. The flame was so bright that the trees at the edge of the clearing appeared to have disappeared.

A blanket of heavy fog folded itself around the outside of the flames, sealing the clearing off from the rest of the world. The mist was a dark grey curtain that reflected the bonfire like a sheet of ancient armor. A troupe of dancers swirled and leapt around the ghostly fire, but they cast no shadows on the ground. Sitting back from the dancers, four drummers sat cross-legged in a circle, their muscular arms going up and down as they beat on a huge drum.

The dancers stamped their feet. Some of them were half-naked, dressed only in buckskin breech cloths and leggings, their long black hair flowing freely down their backs, bouncing in time with their steps. One dancer

114

swayed beneath a heavy buffalo skin, his face covered by the massive head of the animal. He wove back and forth, the buffalo's horns dipping and diving, as he stomped and strutted in time with the drums. Another warrior danced by, his chest plate festooned with porcupine quills, his head piece made of eagle feathers, his moccasins black from prairie ash. He leapt into the air and charged the buffalo dancer, lifting his spear high over his head, then bringing it down on the buffalo's back and rolling away into the maelstrom of warriors that pounded and danced behind him.

Frosty snorted and trumpeted a warning. Charlie and Sal pawed the earth nervously. The horses nickered and drew closer together, but didn't try and run away. Frosty reared, his ears pinned back flat.

"Whoa, Frosty," Hannah commanded.

Frosty reared again, then trotted around the fire. He slid to a stop beside Hannah, his pink nostrils flared, his eyes dangerously bright.

"Oh, no," Johnny groaned, his eyes blinking rapidly.

"Thank God, you're back with us," Hannah said, a hand on Frosty's neck to try and soothe him.

Johnny shook off the last of his trance and looked at his friends. He had no idea why he was dressed and standing by the fire. He turned and gazed into the spirit fire. The dancers wheeled and dipped. He shuddered, his hands trembling. Through sheer will power alone, he was able to keep his teeth from chattering.

"Johnny? What is happening? Who are they?" Hannah asked, her voice shaking.

"I'm still sleeping, aren't I? Someone tell me I am. Either that or we're all hallucinating," Ross quipped, his

115

voice cracking. He wondered what on earth had made him think that seeing a bunch of ghosts would be fun. They should have gone back to town with the rest of the Pumpkin Ride.

"They're Blackfoot," Johnny croaked, his voice a hoarse whisper.

"How can you tell?" Linda squeaked.

"See the dancer with the long ropes of braided sweet grass hanging from his waist? See how he dips and sways like the wind moving across the Prairies? He's a Grass Dancer," Johnny pointed to a tall brave, who danced from side to side, dipping down, then sliding forward and back, imitating the movement of long grasses swaying in the wind. "Look! See that brave with the porcupine roach headpiece and the feather bustle at his back, that symbol painted on his chest is the Thunderbird. He must be a really powerful warrior to wear the Thunderbird. There are even lightning bolts streaking out of it. Look at their moccasins. They are black on the bottom from prairie ash; that's how the Blackfoot got their name."

The warriors danced. Drummers pounded the kettle drum. Tortoise shell rattles rattled. The kids watched in awe as the group of braves jigged and bobbed, mesmerized by the sounds and the sights. The horses snorted and stomped their hooves, almost in time with the drums.

A tall, broad-chested chief with a huge war bonnet of eagle feathers fastened to his head broke away from the fire and walked towards them. As he did, his form grew more solid, the great porcupine quilled sun sewn into his chest plate glowing softly. His soft deer skin leggings and breech cloth were painted with horizontal black lines. Heavy furrows creased the corners of his deeply bronzed

116

skin and a smile twitched at the corners of his mouth. He signaled for the kids to step into the circle, to come and join the Dance.

"He wants us to join them," Linda said, her mouth falling open. She clamped her jaw shut, broke into a big smile, leaned over the rim of stones that marked the Medicine Wheel's edges and reached out to the chief. Ross snatched her hand back, away from the chief's open embrace.

"Linda, what are you doing? Chief War Bonnet is a ghost! Don't touch him. You don't know what he wants or what will happen," Ross gasped. "Hannah, help me out here."

"Look, he's smiling. He wants us to dance with him. He's not going to hurt us. I just know it," Linda said, fixing her brother with a steely look. "I don't know how I know it, I just do."

"Listen to your brother, Linda. You don't know for sure," Hannah agreed, her eyes sparkling, reflecting the blue light of the spirit-fire.

All at once, a fiddle's sharp whine stilled the beating drums. It warbled and whined, refining itself into a toe-tapping Acadian song. The air hummed, the strings meowing out a capering tune. The drums picked up the rhythm.

Dum. Tom. Tom.

The fiddler appeared as if by magic, one minute unseen, the next minute jumping out of the wall of fog behind the spirit-fire as if he had been waiting there all along. He dipped and danced, the fiddle tucked under his chin, his tall leather boots flapping, the red sash around his waist swinging back and forth in time with the music. His crisp white shirt snapped and crackled with every bow and turn. Tilting his head and winking, he motioned for the kids to jump into the fray.

Chief War Bonnet held out a hand once again. Linda squealed with delight and bolted past her brother. She leapt over the ring of stones and grabbed hold of the chief's hand.

"Come on, bro. It's okay," she shouted at her brother.

Chief War Bonnet and Linda walked, hand in hand, across the clearing. Linda laughed and started to dance, stamping the ground with her boots, hopping from one foot to the other, darting in and out of the group of dancing braves like a lunatic. The braves laughed and moved out of her way. The fiddler fiddled in beside her, his eyes bright, a huge smile on his face. The pair danced in circles, around and around each other.

Out of the flames of the bonfire, like a Phoenix rising, a stunningly beautiful woman sashayed, her long hair glistening and her eyes twinkling like a pair of red rubies. She grinned at the fiddler, lifted her black skirt and swirled away amidst the group of braves.

Ross glanced sideways at Johnny and Hannah. "I really don't want to do this, but I have to go. I have to look after my sister."

Hannah nodded, Johnny shivering uncontrollably at her side.

Ross took a deep breath and hurdled himself over the line of stones, lifting his body high into the air, not wanting to tread on them lest the flaming rocks burn his feet. The woman laughed, swung out from behind the backside of the fire and grabbed hold of both of Ross' hands. She dragged him into a close embrace. Ross blushed a deep shade of crimson. She laughed harder and spun him off his feet, whirling him around in ever widening circles.

The fear left Ross' face. He laughed, kicked up his heels, pulled away from the woman and waltzed off with his sister. "Come on. It's fun," he hollered as he and Linda whizzed by.

"Let's go," Hannah said. "Don't be afraid, Johnny."

"I am afraid. I'm Cree. They're Blackfoot," Johnny gasped, pointing at the warriors.

The fiddler broke away from the spirit-fire and walked over to Johnny. He stood on the far side of the stones, tucked the fiddle under one arm and pointed the bow at Johnny. He smiled and nodded encouragement, a tousle of auburn hair falling over his forehead, his brown eyes glinting with elfish glee. He pointed to his sash, then to Johnny's empty waist. The question was clear: where was Johnny's red sash?

"Isn't that a Métis sash that the fiddler's wearing?" Hannah asked. She turned to face Johnny and squeezed his hand. "He wants to know where yours is."

"Yes. That's a Métis sash that he's wearing. He knows...He's pointing at my waist because he knows...," Johnny stammered, his mouth falling open.

"The Blackfoot don't mind him so why should they mind you? And what about your mother, Johnny? She's not Cree."

Johnny fingered the Medicine Bundle that hung around his neck, wondering if his mother would dance with these Ghost Dancers. He suspected she would. He wished she were here to council him.

119

The fiddler waited patiently while Johnny argued with himself.

"Three parts make up a whole. I am Salish, French and Cree! I don't want to turn my back on my people like my father and my grandfather did. My mother would dance with them, I'm sure of it. This Ghost Dance is for all of us," he said to Hannah, his eyes wide in amazement.

"Not all ghosts are scary," Hannah said quietly. "My grandmother walked beside us on the Pumpkin Ride tonight. Sometimes, I think I see her sitting in her old rocker. We keep it on our back porch because Gram loved to sit in it, drink tea, and tell us stories of fairies and sprites. Seeing her like that, walking beside me, that didn't scare me at all."

Hannah lifted a hand and gave Frosty a reassuring pat. The gelding sighed, settling down. Sal snored softly, her head down, not much caring that there were ghosts in the mists. Charlie chewed placidly on a clump of withered rye.

"So shall we dance?"

Johnny grinned, bowed to Hannah and held out a hand, palm up. Hannah curtsied and accepted his hand gracefully.

The fiddler picked up his fiddle, cradled it under his chin and started to play.

The two friends stepped over the stones, arm in arm, and across the boundaries of the Medicine Wheel with only Frosty's liquid eyes to bare witness to their crossing.

Chapter Nine

The Ghost Ride

The stars in the heavens began to wink out as a swirling shroud of cottony mist drifted across the ghostly bonfire causing it to flicker and dim as if a silken veil had been dropped over the flames. Great puffy clouds drifted across the sky, each one large and dense enough to support a whole city. Dawn was fast approaching.

The campfire in front of the cabin had dwindled to a smouldering mound of grey ash. Long neglected, it fed upon itself until there was nothing left to burn. The sleeping bags around its base were damp humps of blue and green nylon, the top layers speckled with water. The saddles too were soaked with morning dew. Behind the fire, the somber light of the early dawn made the old trapper's cabin look sad and empty, a relic long forgotten, its purpose lost in the past.

All at once, the dancers stopped dancing and the drummers stopped drumming. The fiddler tucked his fiddle under his arm and gathered up his beautiful wife.

The couple smiled and bowed to the children, then waved them off.

Chief War Bonnet gathered up the group of friends and pointed first at the sky, then over to the horses who were standing waiting patiently for their masters to return.

"I think the chief wants us to pack up," whispered Ross, his voice coming out small and lonely in the misty morning.

"Yeah. We better go," replied Johnny.

They watched for a moment as the braves drifted into the woods, disappearing like the wraiths they were. They reappeared with ghostly steeds in tow. The ponies were angular and strong, gayly painted with red stripes and yellow hand prints. The horses were of no particular breed or color, some were Appaloosa, other's were paints or solids.

The chief motioned again for the kids to gather up their belongings.

"I think we're supposed to ride with them," ventured Hannah.

"That's great! I don't have a horse. Pizzazz took off, remember?" Ross added, his voice tinged with despair.

"Try calling her," suggested Johnny. "Maybe she didn't go that far."

Ross shrugged. "Guess it can't hurt."

Frosty nickered softly to Hannah, anxious to be on the way home. He stomped a hoof in impatience. Hannah stepped over the stones and outside of the Medicine Wheel. She shook the water off her sleeping bag, rolled it into a tight bundle, and tied her gear to the back of the saddle, not looking forward to sitting on the wet leather. Linda and Johnny followed suit.

"Zazzy!" Ross called. "Pizzazz!"

A far off whinny echoed through the woods.

"Zazzy," he called again.

The ground shook. The brush at the edge of the clearing exploded as Pizzazz burst through it. The mare galloped across the meadow, her tail in the air, clearly happy to have been called. She snorted and skidded to a halt in front of Ross.

"Well I'll be a snookered cowboy," joked Ross.

"See! You didn't need to worry. Pizzazz knew what she was doing," Linda teased her brother. "She just didn't want to dance with no ghosts."

"Come on. We better hurry. The chief is starting to look angry," Hannah said.

Ross looked up and saw that the chief was no longer smiling. He waved again at the heavens, his face a dark scowl, the braves clustered in a tight pack behind him.

The spirit-fire was almost completely invisible now. The flames were just a few small blue sparks that flickered over the grass like a sad version of the Northern Lights.

A tall brave with grey hair walked a chestnut and white paint horse through the middle of the group of braves. The horse was powerfully muscled, with clumps of eagle feathers tied in his mane and golden suns painted on his rump. The chief vaulted gracefully onto the gelding's back, the warriors following suit and reining their ponies in behind him.

The kids quickly tacked up their horses, working in silence, their eyes blood shot and their faces haggard from the long night of dancing.

The horses snorted and pranced; even Sal swished her tail and pricked up her ears. They were well rested and ready to go home. Pizzazz was none the worse for wear for spending a night in the bush.

The chief nodded and walked his horse up the trail the kids had ridden in on. The spirit-fire gave out one final flurry of blue sparks, then died out completely. The Medicine Wheel's stones returned to their normal size, the greyish granite becoming cold and lifeless.

The brave wearing the buffalo cape signaled for Johnny to ride behind the chief. Johnny did as he was told and reined Charlie in behind the paint gelding. The brave then motioned for the other kids to follow. They quickly mimicked Johnny and did as ordered. The rest of the warriors formed a rear guard, the procession stretching all the way back to the cabin's front porch.

The fiddler and his wife walked hand-in-hand beside Johnny. The fiddler's wife had a playful smile on her lips, and her eyes sparkled with life. The fiddler smiled crookedly as if he was party to some amusing joke. That he loved his wife was evident by the soft look in his eye and the jauntiness in his step. Johnny was surprised that Charlie didn't seem to mind their presence.

Frosty and Pizzazz snorted, loving the briskness of the morning.

The soft clip clop of the ponies hooves resonated through the forest. The spruce and cedar trees glistened, their needles dripping with heavy dew. The morning mists swirled in little eddies around the horses' legs, caressing them with wet kisses, and turning their breath to candyfloss. The earth underfoot smelled loamy and slightly rotten, as it does in fall, before the frost sets in.

The forest was still dark, but gradually the trees took shape. The rotting stumps scattered forlornly amidst the stands were covered with layers of thick springy moss.

The Great Pumpkin Ride had left its mark on Pumpkin Alley, the wagons leaving deep ruts in the trail, the roadway a mass of hoof prints from a hundred horses and ponies.

The orange pumpkins were limp and lifeless; the candles nestled deep within the hollowed out flesh were clumps of blackened wax. The pumpkins weren't favorites anymore; they leered and winked at the passing riders.

Johnny turned in his saddle to check on Hannah. Her face was deathly pale and her lips were blue. Johnny could hear her teeth chattering so he reined Charlie in beside Frosty, un-did the woolen blanket tied in a roll on the front of his saddle, shook it out, then draped it over her shoulders. Hannah dropped her reins, tugged it up under her chin and nodded in thanks.

The chief halted the paint gelding at the end of the forest trail, Pumpkin Alley now far behind. The long, muddy wagon trail before him ambled along the cliff top towards town. The white railings of the fairground's riding ring were visible in the distance.

The sky was light grey, swollen to bursting with rain clouds. It started to drizzle, soaking the horses' coats and filling the air with the smell of horse manure and sweet cedar. The Athabasca River gurgled in the valley below.

125

Johnny and his friends reined up beside the chief. One by one, the braves rode by on their brightly painted ponies. They nodded to each of the teens in turn and walked their horses into the forest, fading away into nothingness before the kid's eyes. As each warrior disappeared, so too did the sound of his pony's hoof falls. With a sigh, the forest swallowed the group of braves as if they had never existed.

The fiddler and his wife lifted a hand in farewell, broad smiles on their faces. The chief motioned towards town, then nodded and turned his horse into the forest. The fiddler and his wife walked beside the great paint horse, their forms dwindling until nothing was left but a layer of fog drifting through the trees.

The kids sat on their ponies in the rain, lost in their own thoughts, staring at the empty forest where their ghostly companions had disappeared. All at once, they too raised a hand and waved, then turned their horses for home.

Chapter Ten

The Long Ride Home

The rain came, a white sheet of water that sent small boulders tumbling down the cliff into the river below. The water was dark and muddy, a swirling soup of silt and debris. The wind picked up. Trees rustled. Branches fell to the ground in an endless wave.

The kids hunkered down in their saddles as they road into the driving rain, chins buried deep inside their coat collars, hair plastered to their faces, a look of misery in their eyes. The horses picked up their pace, eager to be home inside a warm barn, hooves splashing through deep and ever-widening puddles. The trail was now slick and muddy.

The River Bend County Fairground appeared before them, the riding ring empty, the barrels still in place, and the ground littered with sodden hamburger wrappers and soft drink cans. The barbeque spits sat forlornly on their racks over mushy coal pits, the air above them reeking of rancid fat and burnt wood. The portable horse stalls were clean, but a large pile of manure sat at one end, the work crews not yet having come in to remove it. The men would appear with tractors and trucks after Sunday Services to deal with the bags of garbage tied neatly in bundles leaning against the concession stand. The fairground would be scrubbed and cleaned, then locked up until the spring.

Johnny and Hannah jogged their horses through the parking lot, Ross and Linda following closely at their heels. Ross kicked Pizzazz forward as they exited the fairground and turned right on Third Street. Linda did the same. The four road abreast of each other down the middle of the street.

The rain eased off into a light drizzle and the kids shrugged off a bit of their tiredness.

"Did that really happen?" asked Ross. "Aren't ghosts supposed to be see-through? They shouldn't be real like that, should they?"

"Of course it was real," Linda replied, her eye sockets swollen and bruised as if she had been in a school yard brawl, her white scalp visible through the thin blond hair plastered to it. "My feet hurt too much to doubt it."

Ross growled at his sister, his own eyes hooded and red-rimmed. Water dripped from the end of his nose and down the sides of his rosy cheeks. He had never felt so miserable in all his life.

Johnny and Hannah chuckled.

The horses' metal shoes clip-clopped loudly on the pavement, the surface black and greasy. The sound was desolate. It reminded the kids that they were still alone.

The shops they rode by were lightless, closed signs hanging on the doors. Drapes were drawn. The image of the four sodden riders, wet and sullen, reflected back at them in the darkened windowpanes.

"Maybe we all ate too much and had the same dream?" Ross offered, still not convinced about what had happened.

"No. It happened. Your sister's right. My foot aches and my stump is throbbing," said Hannah. "I'm going to need a seriously long and hot bath when I get home."

"Yeah. I don't think I've ever been so cold," added Linda, her lips quivering.

"I'd give you Johnny's blanket, but it's soaked. It's not doing me much good anymore."

"That's okay. It won't be long until we get home," Linda said bravely.

Hannah smiled weakly.

The kids rode past the River Bend Grocery Store and the Feed & Seed. No one was about; not a truck or car was on the road this Sunday morning.

"What time do you think it is? I lost my watch. Must be really early 'cause I don't see any lights on in the church yet," Ross commented as they walked their horses by the River Bend Seventh Day Adventist church. The windows in the church were as dark and fathomless as the rest of the town. The potted yellow mum's that lined the outside walkways were bent over from the heavy rains, the petals coated with dirt.

"Must be around six a.m. or six thirty," Johnny figured.

They continued to ride on in silence for a little while, too cold to talk. Their feet were wrinkled prunes inside their boots. The water on their saddles had soaked their jeans from the moment they sat on them an hour earlier.

"You know, I don't think we should tell anybody about what happened last night," Ross said, looking sheepishly at Johnny.

Johnny breathed a sigh of relief, fingering the limp bundle that hung around his neck. He had been wondering how to approach this subject. He was afraid that some of the kids from town might go out and disturb the stones of the Medicine Wheel if they knew about it. It needed to be protected.

"I agree," Johnny said.

"Why not?" whined Linda. She was dying to tell Betty about her new friend, Chief War Bonnet. That was the whole point of the camp-out, being the envy of all her friends.

"Because too many people will go out there. They might destroy the Medicine Wheel," reasoned Hannah, knowing what Johnny was thinking, but not sure about Ross. She reached out and patted Linda's hands, then pulled back from the icy touch. Linda's hands were fish-belly white, whiter even than her own, the skin under the fingernails a faint blueish-purple. Linda was a real trooper, but Hannah knew she needed to get her home quickly.

"Yeah, I guess you're right," Linda sniffed.

"Who's gonna believe us?" Ross smiled at his sister. "I think people will think that we've all gone mad, or are lying, which would be worse."

Linda shrugged, then scowled, clearly unhappy about it.

"I think we better get your sister home as fast as possible, Ross," nodded Hannah.

"You do look pretty blue, Linda. Let's move over to the shoulder and pick up the pace. I'm pretty cold too and it'll warm us up," Johnny said, moving Charlie Horse into the lead.

The kids reined in behind each other and let their horses canter along the highway's sandy shoulder. The rain stopped completely and a heavy mist settled over the tilled fields they passed. Steam rose off the horses' shoulders and butts.

Hannah's gravel driveway came into view around the bend in the highway. She was thrilled to see the white two storey farmhouse with the wide front porch. Frosty nickered and increased his speed.

Johnny reined up at the end of the lane.

"I'll come help you with Frosty, if you like?" he offered.

"Okay. My hands are so numb that I don't know if I can unwrap his cinch," said Hannah gratefully.

"We're gonna head home. I'm hoping Mom's got the griddle on." Ross motioned up the highway. "You sure you don't want to join us, Johnny?" Ross joked, weakly.

Johnny smiled and shook his head.

Ross winked back at him.

"I appreciate you guys deciding to keep this to yourselves. What happened...," stammered Johnny, "was really important to me. I don't know how to describe it. I just feel whole, I guess."

"Cosmo," Linda squeaked, her voice thin. "Can we do it again next year?"

"No!" Ross, Hannah and Johnny exclaimed, then started giggling.

"I think one Ghost Dance in a lifetime is quite enough, Lindy." Ross grinned.

"Party-poopers," Linda quipped.

"Let's go, Lindy."

Ross nodded at Hannah, fired a cheeky grin at Johnny and wheeled Pizzazz around on her haunches. The mare reared slightly. He pressed her into a trot and didn't look back.

"See you on the bus tomorrow," Linda called over her shoulder as Sal let out a short buck and cantered after Pizzazz.

Johnny and Hannah waved, then sat for a moment watching the McClouds ride home. Without comment, they turned Charlie and Frosty up the Storey's lane way. They crossed the front yard, circling Hannah's mother's rose garden, heading for Frosty's barn.

"You want to put Charlie in the barn with Frosty and come in for breakfast? I'll get one of my dad's sweaters for you to warm up in," Hannah ventured.

"Yeah. I'd like that," Johnny said.

Hannah smiled at him; it warmed Johnny's heart.

He glanced at the line of spruce trees in the distance, knowing that as the crow flies, the old trapper's cabin and the Medicine Wheel was only a mile straight north of the Storey's property. He tipped his head in thanks to the Grandfathers. The Blackfoot weren't his ancestors, but they had helped him find peace, a peace that would last him a lifetime.